Dr. Dredd's Wagon of Wonders

DR DREDD'S
WAGON OF
WONDERS

Dr. Dredd's Wagon of Wonders

by Bill Brittain
drawings by Andrew Glass

HarperTrophy®
A Division of HarperCollins*Publishers*

Dr. Dredd's Wagon of Wonders

Library of Congress Cataloging-in-Publication Data
Brittain, Bill.
Dr. Dredd's wagon of wonders.

Summary: In agreeing to make a deal with Dr. Dredd for the services of Bufu the Rainmaker, the drought-stricken town of Coven Tree enters into a devastating struggle with forces of evil.
[1. Supernatural—Fiction] I. Glass, Andrew, ill. II. Title III. Title: Doctor Dredd's wagon of wonders.
PZ7.B78067Dr 1987 [Fic] 86-45775
ISBN 0-06-020713-2
ISBN 0-06-020714-0 (lib. bdg.)
ISBN 0-06-440289-4 (pbk.)

First Harper Trophy edition, 1989.

For brother Bob

Chapters

Dr. Dredd's Wagon of Wonders

CHAPTER ONE

Strangers

Come and sit close by, while I tell you the tale of Dr. Hugo Dredd and of the awful fate that came near to destroying Coven Tree.

Our little village, tucked away up here in this remote corner of New England, takes its name from the huge oak tree—the Coven Tree—where witches used to gather to perform their mystic rites. From time to time Old Satan himself has been known to walk the forests and mountains around here. We seem to dwell near the great barrier separating our commonplace world from that other realm, where fairies and demons hold sway.

Is it any wonder then, that now and again one of those . . . those *things* . . . finds a way to cross that barrier, if only for a short time? Or that it walks among us, almost unrecognized in its human form, to bring wonder and chaos into our lives?

Such a creature, though no one knew it at the beginning, was Dr. Dredd.

Understand, such beings don't appear often. For the most part the good people of Coven Tree are just country folk—farmers, mainly, with a smattering of traders and craftsmen. We govern our lives by the rising and setting of the sun, the planting and harvesting of crops and the changing of seasons. Babies get born, and old people die. We celebrate the one and mourn the other, just like people everywhere.

By the by, my name's Stewart Meade, but most folks call me Stew Meat, and you can, too. I've owned the Coven Tree General Store for more years than I care to remember. Because I've learned to keep my ears open and my mouth shut, I hear a lot of what goes on in our village. And that's about all the introduction you're going to get, so let's go on with the story.

It was April—the spring of the great drought in Coven Tree. To this day, folks speak about that spring like it was a curse laid on the village. There'd been no snow to speak of the winter past, and that meant no water gushing down from off the mountains to fill our creeks and ponds. Rain? None. Each day was like the rest, with the sun hanging in the sky like a disc of polished brass and an arid wind blowing across dusty earth.

Spider Crick, usually full to overflowing, was just a muddy trickle. Wells all over town were running dry, and the water that came up in the buckets was a slimy green. The farmers' fields were baked hard and criss-crossed with a million great cracks, each one like a gaping mouth, crying out with thirst.

It was a bleak time for us all. Farmers couldn't plant their crops, and their livestock were faring poorly in the heat and desert dryness. And in Coven Tree, when the farmers don't prosper, it means hard times for us merchants as well. It was getting to the point where rain—a good, drenching rain of several days' duration—would be more valuable than gold.

I was at my desk in the store one Friday afternoon, balancing my ledgers. The job was too easy for my liking, as customers had been scarce of late. Still, adding those columns of figures made my eyes tired, so I leaned back in my chair and stared out through the window to rest them.

That's when I saw the odd-looking stranger who stood on the dirt road outside.

He was bare to the waist and wore only curious trousers that seemed to be made of a single piece of cloth, wrapped about his waist and held in place by a wide belt. He had not a single hair anywhere on his head or body. At first glance he appeared heavily muscled, with ponderous arms and legs, and a chest the size of a bass drum.

But as he climbed the steps to the store and crossed the porch, he seemed to shrink in upon himself. The arms became thinner, as did the legs. The mighty chest got smaller, and one or two ribs showed beneath the skin.

My thought at the time was that my eyes were playing me false. What walked through my open door was just an average-sized man, though he still wore those funny pants and was as bald as a plucked chicken.

In one hand the man clutched perhaps a dozen placards printed in bold black letters. He lurched across the floor to my desk and extended one of them for my inspection. The placard's lettering was so big I didn't need my glasses to read it:

Dr. Dredd's
WAGON OF WONDERS
***
SEE
The Stuff of Fantasy and Myth
Displayed before Your Eyes!
***
WITNESS
The Mystic Powers of:
ANTAEUS—World's Greatest Wrestler!!
and
BUFU—Miracle Boy of the East!!
***
Come . . . and be AMAZED.
Amusing! Educational!! Provocative!!!

Down at the bottom of the poster, a few more words had been added in pencil:

Free Show
The Clearing, West of Town
Saturday morning, 10 o'clock

"You . . . put . . . poster . . . in . . . store," growled the man like he didn't speak English any too well. "Where . . . everybody . . . see . . . it."

"I'll be glad to," I said, taking the poster. "What with our dry spell, folks need something to take their minds off their troubles. Are you this Dr. Dredd fellow or d'you just work for him?"

He banged a fist against his chest. "I . . . am . . . Antaeus!"

Before I could reply, he was out the door and down the steps. Oddly enough, as soon as his feet hit the ground, he seemed to grow taller and fill out again, with muscles bulging and rippling throughout his body. Perhaps, I thought, my eyes needed looking at.

Antaeus headed for Sven Hensen's blacksmith shop, waving one of the posters like a battle flag. I tacked mine to the front of the counter. If that Antaeus was the world's greatest wrestler, I wasn't about to miss Dr. Dredd's show. We've got some pretty good wrestlers right here in Coven Tree.

Saturday dawned hot and dry, just like every other day that spring. I got an early start for the clearing. As I locked the store and prepared to leave, I couldn't help wondering why Dr. Dredd would give a show and not charge for it. Still, if the man was a fool, it wasn't my place to remind him of that fact.

The wagon stood right in the center of the clearing. It was perhaps twenty feet long, with windows along each side. Green paint was peeling from the boards, which were warped and had gaps between them. From two poles that stuck up from the roof hung a banner of dirty canvas that bore the faded message:

Dr. Dredd's Wagon of Wonders

At the front, the wagon tongue had been turned aside to make room for a set of steps leading up to a door. At the rear was a second door, cracked and aslant. Here a small platform had been rigged up like a little stage, with steps leading down to the ground. Over to one side, two swaybacked horses munched grass near a tent.

Not very impressive, I thought.

During the next couple of hours more and more people came trickling into the clearing until about everybody in town was there. Dressed in everything from overalls to Sunday best, they all seemed to be waiting for something to happen.

I overheard Sumner Beezum, who fancies himself to be something of a wit, talking with Eli Phipps, our mayor. "I took a peek in the tent," Sumner told Eli. "Three bedrolls inside, but nobody about. D'you reckon the good Dr. Dredd and his troop crawled inside that wagon and just died?" He gave a cackling laugh that sounded like a turkey gobbling.

Another fifteen minutes passed. I got around to saying hello to Dan'l and Jenny Pitt, and the Fiske family. Sven Hensen, the big blacksmith, was there, fingering his necktie like it was choking him. Sheriff Roscoe Houck looked important as all get-out, with his silver badge flashing in the sunlight.

"Howdy, Stew Meat," said a girl's voice.

It was Ellen McCabe, looking pretty as a picture in a new dress she must have made herself. Just fourteen, she was turning into a fine young woman.

"Howdy, Ellen," I replied. "Where's your folks?"

"Daddy's in Boston, talking to some bankers and trying to get a loan to tide us over this dry spell, and Mama didn't want to see the show without him. At first, she didn't want me to come either. But I sort of talked her into it."

That was Ellen, all right. Once she got her mind set on something, she'd find a way to do it, no matter what.

"If you're alone, I'd be honored if you'd see the show with me, fair lady," I said, offering my arm like a fancy gentleman.

"Why thank you, kind sir," she said, curtseying low. Then we both laughed at the airs we were putting on.

Another fifteen minutes went by. Finally a shout came from a woman in the crowd. "Bring on the show!"

The words were no sooner out of her mouth than the rear door of the wagon banged open. After a chorus of *ahhh*s and *ohhh*s, everybody was still. We stared at the strange man who'd stepped out into the sunlight.

He was well over six feet tall and as gaunt as a dead tree limb. A suit of black wool hung on him like wash on a line, and a string tie of the same color looped down across his shirtfront. On his head was a tall hat of red silk, and in his right hand he clutched a coiled whip of braided leather.

His eyes were almost hidden beneath a ridge of brow, and his nose was long and thin, like the beak of a hawk. The cruel slash of mouth put me in mind of a snapping turtle awaiting its prey. His left hand kept moving back and forth across his chest, the fingers ever in motion like the legs of some huge spider.

For some time he turned his head this way and that as if inspecting the assembled people, who were awed and silent in his presence. Finally he uncoiled his whip, and with swift jerks of his arm he cracked it over the heads of his audience. Once . . . twice . . . thrice . . .

While the sharp cracks of the whip still echoed from the surrounding hills, the sinister-looking man started to speak.

"Ladies and gentlemen, I am Dr. Hugo Dredd. I bid

you welcome to this free exposition of my Wagon of Wonders."

"What wonders?" bawled somebody.

"You may well ask," replied Dr. Dredd. "Inside this wagon is the stuff of fantasy and myth . . . and nightmare. Perhaps, for example, you believe the unicorn to be a creature only of fable. Come inside and observe its skull.

"The mirror of Calchas, soothsayer for the Greeks at the Trojan War, awaits your inspection too. In the mirror one can behold dreams and desires locked deep within one's soul and never uttered aloud. You'll also see the mermaid, the egg of the Great Chinese Dragon, the sword of Achilles. And of interest to all is the armor belonging to the Black Knight of Etherium."

"The *who*?" Ellen cried out.

"Many centuries ago," Dr. Dredd intoned in a hollow voice, "the Black Knight of Etherium terrorized most of Europe, bringing low whole armies. He seemed impossible to defeat. It was said his mighty sword could cleave through the stoutest wood and the hardest stone."

"Was he never bested?" I asked.

"Not in battle, sir. A simple jester brought him to ruination by discovering his best-kept secret. Yet 'tis said"—Dredd's voice became low and ominous—"that the Black Knight's spirit still exists within the armor you will see inside."

"Sounds to me, Dr. Dredd, like you've been sampling Curley Weisert's applejack!" hooted Sumner Beezum. "Two drinks of that, and you'll believe most anything."

"You may scoff now," replied Dr. Dredd. "But when you see what awesome marvels my wagon contains, you'll sing a different tune."

POP the whip cracked once again. "Step up, step up, ladies and gentlemen. It's free, you know. Come now, who'll be first?"

With that, everybody began crowding around the rear of the wagon. Dr. Dredd assisted a couple of old folks in climbing the steps and then scuttled back inside. Ellen and I found ourselves swept along by the milling people, and within a couple of minutes we were inside the dimly lit wagon.

The first thing I saw, propped in a corner, was the

top half of a suit of armor, all black and gleaming.

"Seems the bottom part is missing," I told Dredd, who stood nearby.

"It's at the far end of the wagon," he replied. "Legend has it that if the two sections of the armor were to be joined, the Black Knight would rise again to scourge the countryside."

"Do you believe that, Stew Meat?" Ellen whispered. I shook my head.

"Next," Dredd went on, "the skull of the fabled unicorn."

Dredd pointed to what at first seemed to be the skull of a horse lying on a table. But protruding from the skull's forehead was a horn near two feet in length, with a spiral groove running from end to end.

"Prob'ly carved out of wood," said Sumner Beezum, "and glued to a horse's head."

Ellen ran her fingers along the horn. "Mighty good job of gluing," she said. "It's planted firm, like it grew there. And it sure feels a lot more like bone than wood."

We shuffled our way past a great bronze sword, which, according to Dredd, Achilles himself had wielded in the Trojan War. Next to it was a mummified paw, supposedly from the Sphinx, a monster with the head of a woman and the body of a lion.

The mirror of Calchas the soothsayer was next. It was a simple circle of polished silver in a frame of dark wood. Dr. Dredd seemed particularly anxious that each person who passed should have a chance to peer long and carefully into it.

When it came my turn, I looked and saw my face, of course, and the people standing around me. But then, in some eerie fashion, the mirror image seemed to waver and change. I imagined I saw myself wearing expensive clothes and sitting at a desk of polished wood, as broad as a barn door, in a fancy office. On one wall, in bronze letters, were the words MEADE'S FAMOUS DEPARTMENT STORE.

Within the depths of the mirror I was rich and prosperous and . . .

Reluctantly I jerked my eyes away from my own image.

Near the end of the wagon, in a glass jar of clear liquid, floated something with the head and body of a human babe and the nether parts of a fish. An infant mermaid that had died when pulled from the sea in a fisherman's net, explained Dredd.

Finally, just by the exit door and near a piece of rotting wood that was supposed to have come from the Trojan Horse, was Dredd's last marvel.

"Here you see an egg of the Great Chinese Dragon, my proudest possession," he said. "At great personal risk I took it from the highest mountains of Mongolia and smuggled it out of the country. Feel it, feel it! Note how warm it is. The creature inside still lives!"

The egg, nearly as large as a gallon jug, looked to be an oval rock of the blackest stone, all polished and gleaming. I laid my hand on it. It was warm all right, though you'd expect rock to be cool to the touch. And oddly enough the thing seemed to throb under my fingers like a beating heart.

Then, after a quick glance at the leg pieces of the armor of the Black Knight, Ellen McCabe and I walked out into the sunlight. "What do you think, Stew Meat?" she asked me. "Can any of that stuff be what it's said to be?"

"If you'd asked me that ten minutes ago," I said,

"I'd have laughed in your face. But inside that spooky wagon, with Dredd giving his little speeches . . . well, it was a mighty convincing show."

"Well, lookin' in that mirror sent shivers through me," said Ellen. "It was eerie, I tell you."

It certainly was, I thought. But I kept silent, not wanting to frighten the girl more than she was already.

It took more'n an hour for everybody to make their way through Dr. Dredd's Wagon of Wonders. Finally the last of the people came outside, and we all gathered around the rear of the wagon. We hadn't forgotten what else the posters had promised.

Again Dredd came out onto the platform. With him was Antaeus, who'd brought the poster to my store. Now, in the sunlight, he appeared of only average size.

"The mighty Antaeus!" Dredd announced. "Wrestler of myth, and wrestler supreme! Clear a space down there so he may show his incredible power and skill."

The crowd formed a kind of a circle, perhaps twenty feet across. Dredd raised his hands for silence.

"Now then, who'll challenge my fighter?"

Several of the young men raised their hands. I had to admit, Antaeus didn't look all that hard to beat.

"Let not the weak and puny apply," said Dredd with a chuckle, "for Antaeus has never been bested since joining my show. I call on your biggest and bravest fighter."

"Sven Hensen's the strongest man in Coven Tree!" someone cried out. "Let him fight!"

All eyes turned to Sven. The blacksmith, however, shook his head firmly. "I don't gonna fight joost for sport," he said.

"A wise decision, sir," said Dredd. "But is there no one else?"

"Me!"

Packer Vickery came ponderously forward. The ground trembled and shuddered at each step. Packer was more a mountain than a man. He weighed some three hundred pounds.

"All Packer'll have to do is lay down on that Antaeus," bawled Sumner Beezum, "and he'll never move until Packer lets him up."

"Don't be too sure," said Dredd. "Sometimes the eyes play tricks on the mind." He gestured with his whip, and Antaeus came down from the platform. One bare foot touched the ground. Then the other.

As if something inside him were struggling outward, Antaeus seemed to expand. He grew a full three inches taller. Muscles surged and bulged in shoulders and torso and arms and legs. Suddenly the thing standing at the bottom of the platform steps seemed more monster than human.

"Ohhhh!" gasped the crowd, unable to believe their eyes.

"But that's not the same . . ." Packer Vickery began.

"Afraid?" scoffed Dredd. "Come, come, Mr. Vickery. Would you have us believe that anyone your size is something *less* than a man?"

As Dredd continued talking, Antaeus began flexing his huge muscles. He looked to his right and left and seemed to delight in the astonished murmurings from the throng.

Suddenly Packer Vickery plunged forward at a speed I'd not thought a man of his bulk could possess. He slammed his great weight into Antaeus's massive belly like a runaway locomotive.

Caught unawares, Dredd's wrestler toppled backward, with Packer clutching him in a bearlike embrace. The two men thudded to the ground, and the sound was that of a mighty oak tree being felled. For a moment they lay still, with Packer's great weight pressing down on his astonished opponent's chest and shoulders.

"Count of three?" panted Packer, turning his head to look up at Dredd. "That's all it'll take to lick your man?"

Dredd nodded. Packer began counting.

"One! Two! Thr—— Ohhhh!"

Packer's cry of surprise was echoed by several people in the crowd. Antaeus had placed his hands at each side of Packer's massive waist, where they sank deep into the blubbery flesh.

Then Antaeus lifted.

Packer Vickery hung suspended in the air like some great fat bird. Antaeus held him there for a moment. Then, incredibly, the wrestler *threw* Packer away from him and sprang to his feet.

Packer landed on his back with a thud. Before he could get up, his opponent was on him. Antaeus's arms and legs seemed almost glued to the earth as he pulled himself down on top of the stunned Packer Vickery.

"One . . . two . . . three!" cried Dr. Dredd.

Almost before it had begun, the match was over.

People chattered in wonder and excitement at Antaeus's power. Dredd looked this way and that, and there was a crooked smile on his face as if he were savoring Antaeus's victory. Finally he cracked his whip twice. The crowd lapsed into silence.

"Our final feature," Dredd announced, "is Bufu, the Rainmaker."

Rainmaker? Everyone stared at Dredd. Rain? After our long spell of dry weather, even the word sounded strange.

"If this-here Bufu can make it rain, mister, it'll be more wonderful than anything you've got in that wagon," said Sumner Beezum.

Dredd looked around, and his smile changed to a sneer, showing crooked teeth. "Bufu, the Rainmaker!" he repeated, pointing to the door of the wagon.

Nothing happened.

"Bufu!" roared Dredd. "Come out here!"

Still nothing.

Dredd's face twisted into a furious scowl. He rushed into the wagon, slamming the door behind him.

Being curious, I sidled over near one of the wagon's windows. It was open an inch or two. Suddenly I heard a sound that made me start in surprise. There was no mistaking what it was.

It was the splat of a whip striking bare flesh. And it was followed by a sharp cry of pain.

"Hiding under the table again, were you?" I heard Dredd say in a raspy voice. "You get outside, you little wretch. Get out there or I'll take the very skin right off your back!"

CHAPTER TWO

Striking a Deal

"Stew Meat!"

I felt a tug at my sleeve. There was Ellen, staring at the window. Her hand was at her mouth, as if she were frightened, but at the same time her eyes flashed angrily. "Somebody in there is getting beaten," she whispered. "With a whip."

"It's none of our affair, Ellen," I said, more to protect her than because I believed what I was saying.

"It is too! Nobody's got a right to use a whip on

another person. I sure don't aim to just stand here while someone's getting hurt. I'm going in there and . . ."

Before she could say any more, the rear door of the wagon banged open, and out came Dr. Dredd. He was half leading, half dragging a skinny lad of perhaps fifteen or so.

The boy had the swarthy skin of a native of some Eastern country. Strangely enough, though, his eyes were blue. He wore a turban and a green cloak covered with stars, pentagrams and other cabalistic designs. I had little doubt this was Bufu.

While the boy cowered in a corner of the platform, Dr. Dredd stepped forward and looked down at the crowd. "Bufu, the Rainmaker!" he announced once more in a loud voice.

Everybody in the clearing started babbling at one another at once. The sound grew and grew until it was a great hum, like a gigantic swarm of bees. On everybody's lips was the same word: *Rain!*

"There's no rain up in that sky," hooted Sumner Beezum. It was true. The sky was a brilliant blue, and heat waves shimmered on the horizon.

"Ahh," crowed Dr. Dredd. "A doubter. But in five

minutes, you'll wish you'd brought your umbrella, Mr. Beezum."

Funny . . . I hadn't heard Sumner tell Dr. Dredd his name.

Dredd turned to the boy. "Rain!" he snarled. "Now!"

He began uncoiling the whip in his hand.

Trembling all over, the boy came to the middle of the platform. He raised his hands to grip the sides of his head. His eyes shut tight, and his face screwed up into a look of awful pain. He seemed to be working at something with all his might.

A murmur of surprise rippled through the crowd. Beside me, Ellen McCabe pointed upward. I raised my head.

A small cloud had suddenly appeared right above the clearing. Each second it got darker against the blue sky.

Bufu sank to his knees and little moans escaped from his lips.

The cloud was now an inky black. A wind rose. People began clutching at their clothing.

SPUT

The first raindrop hit Mayor Eli Phipps right on top

of his bald head. A few more hit others in the audience. Within seconds there was a heavy downpour, drenching everybody in the clearing.

But we didn't mind—no sirree! Faces turned upward into the driving rain, and outstretched hands tried to catch each precious drop. All over the place, folks were hugging one another and dancing for joy and shouting "Praise be!" and such things. Soaked to the skin, they were all as happy as hogs in mud time.

I guess only a few of us noticed that it was raining *only* above the clearing. On all sides of us, the sky was still clear and blue.

Then, as quickly as it had begun, the rain stopped. Antaeus jerked Bufu inside the wagon again while Dr. Dredd smiled triumphantly down on the people of Coven Tree.

"With that, the free show ends," he said. A big moan of disappointment greeted this announcement. "More rain!" yelled somebody.

"No, that's all there is," said Dredd. "Now we must be on our way." He turned and opened the wagon door.

"Wait!" Mayor Eli Phipps was elbowing his way

through the crush of people and heading toward the platform. "Can . . . can the boy do that—make it rain, I mean—whenever he wants to?"

"Anytime—any place," said Dredd over his shoulder. "But I really must be going on to . . ."

"Could he make it rain for a long time? For a week or two, maybe?" Mayor Phipps asked.

"For as long as you like. But only at my command." Dredd took a step into the wagon.

"Sir," said the mayor in his deepest and grandest voice, "you must not leave us. We have need of you."

Dr. Dredd turned around and came back to the edge of the platform. His toothy smile grew even wider. "A man of goodwill like myself," he said, his voice hissing like a snake, "could hardly desert anyone in need. What is it you want of me, Mayor Phipps?"

"I want . . . we all want . . . rain. If you—and Bufu—can bring it, why, I'm sure we could work out some kind of a deal."

"A deal? I'm always ready to make a deal."

"Then perhaps you'd meet me at my office in the village hall. Today. Within the hour, if you can."

Dredd spread his hands wide. "Certainly, Mayor Phipps. As soon as I give instructions to Antaeus and see that Bufu is taken care of, I'll be at your service."

As the people cheered and clapped, Dredd disappeared inside the wagon. Mayor Phipps looked about, real proud of what he'd done. He spotted me almost at once.

"Stew Meat, I need you," he said, sidling up to me.

"What for, Mayor?"

"It's not hard to see how bad we need rain around here. And I expect that to bring it, Dredd will drive a hard bargain indeed. You're a storekeeper, and you're better at bargaining than anybody else in Coven Tree. I'd like you there to strike the deal with Dredd."

"Whatever you say, Eli. I guess rain'll be worth whatever it costs."

If I'd known then what Dr. Hugo Dredd was really up to, I'd have swallowed my tongue rather than utter that last remark.

Mayor Eli Phipps leaned back in his big padded chair and put his hands flat on his polished desk. I was seated at the end of the desk, but my chair was as hard as a hunk of New England granite.

"Dr. Dredd will be along anytime now," I said, glancing at the clock on the office wall. "So I think we ought to work things out between us about how we'll handle the deal."

"I'll go along with whatever you say, Stew Meat," said the mayor.

"Then let me do all the dickering. This Dredd seems like one smart fellow, and I don't want you gumming things up just when I think I've struck a bargain."

"But Stew Meat, what if Dredd asks for more than the village can afford? I'd have to say something then."

"No, you wouldn't. Tell you what, Eli. If you're pleased with the way things are going, just give a tug at your right ear. And if you figure I'm too high, then haul away at your left one. Got that?"

Mayor Phipps thought about this. "Left ear, everything's okay," he said. "Right ear, it's too—"

"No, the other way around. And one other thing. If you get to saying something I think is better left unsaid, I'm going to rub my nose. Like this." I pressed a finger against the side of my nose.

"I've got it, Stew Meat."

"Then I guess we're ready whenever Dr. Dredd gets here."

As if I'd given a signal, there came three loud raps at the office door. "Come in!" called the mayor.

The big door opened, and Dr. Dredd strode into the room. He was so tall that his high hat almost brushed the ceiling. In one hand was the black whip, coiled and glistening like a snake.

"Please sit down, Dr. Dredd," said the mayor.

"I prefer to stand."

"This here's Stewart Meade," said Eli. "He's my special assistant in charge of . . ."

"Are you having a joke at my expense, Mayor Phipps?" asked Dredd. "Mr. Meade—or Stew Meat, as he's known hereabouts—is the village storekeeper. He's here only to haggle with me over the best terms for bringing rain to Coven Tree."

"You surely know more about us than we do of you, Dr. Dredd," I said, shaking my head in astonishment.

"I make it my business to know about those with whom I have dealings," he replied. "But I assure you both that I intend to be quite reasonable."

Oh, oh! When a bargaining man says he's going to be reasonable, that's the time to grab your purse or wallet in both hands and hang on tight! I didn't let on how worried I was, though. I just made a grin to match the one on Dr. Dredd's face.

"Well," I began, "rain in these parts has been a bit short of late."

Dredd's smile got even wider. "You talk, Stew Meat, as if a gentle shower of an hour or two would solve all your problems. Through the window, however, I see a countryside as parched as desert sand. You need a week of steady rain at the very least to bring life back to your fields."

"And . . . and you can bring that rain," said Mayor Phipps eagerly. Much *too* eagerly, I thought. I rubbed my nose, and Eli quieted down.

"I could, perhaps, call on Bufu to . . ." Dredd continued.

"Maybe we ought to be talking to Bufu himself," I put in, trying to regain the upper hand. "And just leave you out of it."

"Bufu is my servant, and he does only my bidding," replied Dredd smoothly.

"I see." By this time my stomach was all tied up in knots. We were about to get skinned. I was sure of that. But as yet, Dr. Dredd had said nothing about what he wanted.

"What we had in mind was about ten days of rain. Could Bufu handle that?"

"Easily," said Dredd.

"Are you sure?' I demanded. "I'd hate to get everything settled only to find that rain this morning was just a coincidence."

"Coincidence?" Dredd's voice was slicker'n a handful of lard. "What I promise, I deliver. Just as I did for the people of Mapleton."

"Mapleton?" I asked. "The village down in New Hampshire?"

"The same."

"Just what did you do in Mapleton?" Eli asked.

"Two years ago they wanted a railroad spur laid to the center of town, a distance of some five miles. But two of the miles were covered with hardwood forest, and a way had to be cleared through it. 'Twould have taken a team of axmen months to do the job. Far too long. So they dealt with me. And I had a right-of-way cleared through the forest in a single night—a single night! Each tree cut off at the ground as cleanly as a sharp scythe cuts down a stalk of wheat. So give me no more of 'coincidence,' Stew Meat."

Then Dredd paused and shrugged his shoulders. "But I toot my own horn far too loudly," he went on. "What are you prepared to give for ten days of rain?"

"How about . . . say . . . twenty dollars," I said. Mayor Phipps tugged his right ear vigorously. Dredd just chuckled and shook his head.

"Maybe I didn't make myself clear," I continued. "I was thinking of twenty dollars per *day*. That's two hundred dollars total."

Eli still had his hand to his right ear. But he wasn't tugging as strongly anymore.

Dredd continued to shake his head.

"Four hundred?"

No.

"Six hundred?"

No.

"Seven hundred and fifty?"

No.

By this time, Mayor Phipps had taken his hand from

his right ear and was yanking on the left one more and more urgently. "Stew Meat, don't you think we should . . ." he began. But I stroked my nose hard enough to take the skin off the side of it.

Finally I made the offer I'd been leading up to all the time. I figured it'd take Dredd's breath away and still be what Coven Tree could afford if we all tightened our belts a bit. I got to my feet, looked Dredd straight in the eyes and pounded the mayor's desk with my fist.

"One thousand dollars!" I exclaimed.

Dr. Dredd merely shook his head back and forth once more.

I looked at the mayor and shrugged. "I've done my best, Eli," I said. "More'n that, and the whole village will be in the poorhouse, rain or no rain."

"Mebbe if we threw in a few chickens or a side of beef . . ." the mayor said.

"Gentlemen, please." Dr. Dredd spread his arms wide. "You misunderstand me. I'm agreeable to giving you the rain you need. But I want neither your money nor your livestock."

I looked blankly at Eli, and he stared back at me in surprise. "You mean you'll have Bufu make it rain and . . . and you won't charge us *anything*?" the mayor gasped.

"Oh, I might require some small recompense," said Dredd.

"Like what?" I demanded. "I don't like any deal where the terms aren't understood in advance."

"Come, come, Stew Meat," Dredd chided me. "You're far too suspicious. I merely want to do something to—or rather, for—the village of Coven Tree. I've already assured you I'll ask neither cash nor barter."

"But what else could you want?"

"So many questions," said Dredd with a sigh. "Why must we talk of my fee when your village has such need of my services?"

"I still think we should know . . ."

"Stew Meat, shut up!" the mayor ordered. "If this man is such a durned foo—— I mean, such a fine person as to bring us rain, who are we to turn him down?"

I had the feeling deep inside that something was

wrong. Still, Dr. Dredd might be just a man who wanted to do good. And we *did* need rain, that much was certain.

"Do we have a deal, Mayor Phipps?" Dredd laid his whip on the desk and stretched out a hand.

"Done!" With a smile of triumph, Eli grasped Dredd's hand and shook it, sealing the bargain. "Dr. Dredd, it's been a pleasure doing business with you."

Dredd turned on his heel and strode toward the office door. "May you always think so, Mayor Phipps," he said over his shoulder. "May you always think so."

That evening, Ellen McCabe sat with her mother in the kitchen of their little farmhouse at the edge of Coven Tree. "It was ever so wonderful, Mama," Ellen said as she told for the fourth time about the marvels she'd seen that morning. "With the dragon's egg and the wrestling and all."

"I expect it was," replied Mrs. McCabe. "Though your yarn about the boy making rain was a bit hard to swallow. And as for your looking in a mirror and seeing yourself all togged out like a princess, why—"

"But it's all true," Ellen replied.

"Hogwash," snorted Mrs. McCabe. "A giddy girl like you could look at the bottom of a polished pot and see anything she wanted to."

"Oh, pooh, Mama!"

Before Ellen could go on, there was a squawking of chickens from the henhouse. At the same time two of the cows in the barn began bellowing.

"Something's not right out there," said Mrs. McCabe. "All the animals are restless. I don't know if it's a fox trying to get in among the chicks or a snake in the cows' feed bin. I've been out there twice, but I can't find anything. Ellen, you go take a look."

"You just don't want me talking about that mirror anymore," said Ellen. But she took up the lantern from the kitchen shelf, lit it and walked out into the back yard.

In the barn she found that the cows had plenty of hay and there were no snakes about. She patted and soothed them as best she could before heading for the henhouse.

The chickens all seemed safe and snug on their

roosts. But they clucked and prattled more than they had any right to. There's no figuring chickens, Ellen thought.

So as not to waste the trip outside, she decided to bring in a few sticks of stove wood from the shed next to the barn. That way, she wouldn't have to do it in the morning.

She opened the shed's squeaky door and had just grasped a couple of sticks of wood when she heard a rustling sound in the far corner. She wanted to run off, slamming the shed door tight behind her. Instead, she raised the lantern high.

There in the gloom sat a boy about her own age. The shirt he wore was stained with sweat, and his pants had a big rip in one knee. From the looks of him, he'd been crying. He reminded her of one of the wild forest critters she sometimes nursed when they were hurt.

Ellen couldn't help pitying the boy. Besides, if he tried anything bad, she had only to yell once, and Mama would be out with the shotgun.

Ellen held the lantern closer to the boy's face, and a little gasp of surprise came from her lips. "You're

that Bufu, aren't you?" she whispered. "From Dr. Dredd's show."

The boy squirmed farther back into the corner of the shed.

"Come out here this instant!" Ellen snapped. "I know you understand what I'm saying, even if you are a foreigner."

Reluctantly the boy hauled himself out of the corner and inched his way across the shifting hunks of wood. "I ain't no foreigner," he said in a mournful voice. "And my name's not Bufu, either."

As he came nearer, Ellen saw for the first time where his tears had made white streaks along his cheeks, washing away the dark stain that had been scrubbed into his skin.

"Dr. Dredd called you Bufu this morning," she exclaimed in surprise. "If that's not your name, then what . . ."

"I'm Calvin Huckabee. And I come from Vermont. This is the farthest I've ever been away from home in my life. And I don't never want to hear that name Bufu again, so long as I live!"

CHAPTER THREE

Calvin

"Now that you've found me, I guess I'll have to be moving on," Calvin said, peering at Ellen through the gloom of the woodshed.

"No you won't," replied Ellen with a shake of her head. "Right now, you're not going any farther than our house there."

"Are . . . are you planning on turning me over to the law?" Calvin asked in a whispery voice.

"Hmmph! I don't reckon hiding out in our woodshed

with a hole in your britches makes you a real desperate criminal. You just come along now, before I get my dander up."

A little smile flitted across Calvin's face. "You can't make me. I'm bigger'n you are."

"You're sounding just like those uppity boys at school, always trying to be so mean and tough," said Ellen. "But if I was to lay a chunk of this wood alongside your head, hard as I could, I bet you wouldn't be so high and mighty then. Is that what you're wanting?"

"I think I'd rather walk," said Calvin. He scrabbled his way over the pile of wood and stood in the shed's doorway. "D'you live there all alone?"

"Nope. My mama's just inside the kitchen. And if I'm not back pretty quick, she'll come searching. So get a move on."

As the kitchen door opened, Mrs. McCabe looked up from the sink where she had been scrubbing bread pans. Calvin entered sheepishly, followed by Ellen.

"Who's this?" Mrs. McCabe asked in surprise. "Some chicken thief? Or was he stealing milk from the cows? Don't you try nothin', mister. I'd as soon—"

"This here's Bufu, Mama," explained Ellen excitedly. "He's the boy I told you about—the rainmaker from Dr. Dredd's show. Only his real name's Calvin Huckabee and he's running away and he was hiding in our woodshed and I found him and . . . and . . ."

"Have done, Ellen!" ordered Mrs. McCabe. She looked Calvin up and down. "A runaway, eh? Well, you're not the first lad who's left home to go off with a circus or a traveling show only to be sorry afterward. Where do your folks live?"

"I . . . I ain't got no folks. They died some six years back."

Mrs. McCabe shook her head sadly. "I see. And does Dr. Dredd have any claim on you? Is he a relative or such?"

"No, ma'am," said Calvin meekly.

"Then it appears you need to do some explaining as to just what your situation is," said Mrs. McCabe. "But first we'd best feed you. You're thin as a rake. Ellen, you fetch the loaf of bread from the pantry. Slice a goodly portion from the ham in there, too. Then get the sewing box. That tear in Calvin's pants needs mending. And you, Calvin, strip off that shirt. It's filthy enough to stand up alone. I've got a sink full of soapsuds anyway, so I might as well give it a good scrubbing."

Calvin gingerly peeled off his shirt. He turned to put it in the sink behind him.

"Land sakes, boy!" cried Mrs. McCabe, staring at his back. "You've got a bloody stripe across your ribs near as deep as a plowed furrow. How'd that happen?"

"Dr. Dredd, he . . . he hit me with his whip this morning. Just the once, but it does hurt some." Calvin's lower lip began trembling.

"Umm. Sounds to me like there's more to this runaway business than I first thought. I'll want to hear the whole story presently. But first, where's my can of chicken fat?"

In short order Calvin found himself on a kitchen chair, munching a sandwich nearly as thick as it was wide. Ellen was on her knees, mending the rip in his pants with small, neat stitches while her mother rubbed soothing grease onto the slash on his back.

" 'Tain't the first time you was whipped," said Mrs.

McCabe. "I never saw so many scars in my life."

"Dr. Dredd says I've got to learn to mind him better. And the whip's the only thing that'll teach me."

"I'd like to give that awful man a taste of his own medicine," growled Ellen.

"That'll have to wait until another time," replied her mother. "Calvin, how'd you get hooked up with this Dredd fellow, anyway?"

"He wanted me in his show because I can bring rain whenever I want."

"Pshaw!" scoffed Mrs. McCabe. "Nobody can do that."

"I can, ma'am. Mebbe it's because I was born on All Hallows' Eve, just at midnight in the full of the moon. 'Course I never found out about my power until after Ma and Pa had . . . had . . ."

"How'd your folks die, Calvin?" asked Mrs. McCabe gently.

"Chills and fever. It was on a Saturday they began feeling a bit sickly, and two days after that, they were gone. Then I got sent to the orphanage. That's where I found out I could make it rain."

Ellen sat down on a low stool and wrapped her arms about her knees. "Tell us how you found out, Calvin," she said.

"There was a gang of boys at the orphanage who were all bigger and stronger than me, and bullies besides. Miz Lackpin—she ran the place—was always busy, and never saw what was going on. Those boys tormented me something fierce."

"But what's that got to do with the rain?" asked Mrs. McCabe.

"One day there was to be a big party. I'd been looking forward to it for weeks. But on party day, when I went to dress up, I found my clothes all soaked with water and tied in hard knots. With nothing to wear, I had to stay in bed while everyone else was outside in the sunshine, having fun."

Ellen shook her head in sympathy. "I bet you'd have done anything to get even," she said.

"I didn't know what to do. I just lay there in bed making up pictures of those boys in my head. They was trapped under big piles of damp, rotting wood, or standing in pools of green, slimy water with rats swimming all about 'em, or drowning in a pond, with the bottom just too deep for their feet to reach. Then my head began pounding with pain.

"About then, water began pelting down on the orphanage roof, and I heard everybody out at the party begin shouting and hollering. I wrapped myself in a blanket and went to the window."

"And what did you see, Calvin?" asked Ellen.

"There was this big cloud hanging right over the front lawn. Rain was coming down like it was being poured out of buckets. Everybody's clothes were soaked. Their shoes were full of water. Paper plates were floating around like little boats."

"You fixed 'em," said Mrs. McCabe with a chuckle.

"That first time, I didn't know it was me. But when next I got picked on or left out, I began thinking those same thoughts. Then my head would ache and the rain would come. After about the fifth baseball game or picnic I wasn't in on got rained out, everybody began to get the idea. Pick on Calvin Huckabee, and you're going to get wet. The power surprised me as much as anybody else. But I practiced the rainmaking until I got real good at it and could make rain even when I wasn't mad at anybody."

"But how did you get from the orphanage into Dr. Dredd's show?" asked Ellen.

"He came to the orphanage about three years back. I guess the word had gotten out about what I could do. Dredd said he'd take me with him and see to my upbringing. At first, Miz Lackpin wouldn't hear of it, for Dredd had no wife and no real home except for that wagon of his."

By this time, Mrs. McCabe was as caught up in the story as Ellen. "What made her change her mind, Calvin?"

"The oddest thing. Dredd and her went into the office, leaving me outside. But I could hear 'em—or at least I could hear Dr. Dredd. His voice was real low, like wind moaning through the treetops, and he was speaking in a language I'd never heard before. The sound almost put me to sleep. Miz Lackpin didn't say a word, far as I know. But when they came out, she had this dazed look on her face, like she was just waking up. She agreed I was to go with Dr. Dredd. So

I belonged to him, just like that. At the time, I was glad to get away.

"Not anymore, though. I get beaten for the smallest things, and my supper is scraps that Antaeus doesn't want to eat, and making all that rain gets my head to hurting so I can't stand it. I tried running off once or twice. But Dr. Dredd seems able to find me, wherever I go. Then he drags me back and has Antaeus punish me."

"Antaeus?" said Ellen. "The big wrestler?"

"Yep. He's nearly as spooky as Dr. Dredd himself. Just ordinary size when he's up driving the horses or working on the wagon. But as soon as his feet touch the earth, he grows huge and stronger'n any mortal man. Dr. Dredd says Antaeus is almost older'n time itself. And the only person who ever licked him was Hercules."

"That's a strange lot you got yourself mixed up with," said Mrs. McCabe. "You're well rid of them, Calvin. You can stay here a few days, just until we can decide what's to become of you."

"But Dr. Dredd will be looking for me. I've got to

keep moving on. It'd be dangerous for you to hide me."

"You'll stay," said Ellen positively. "And we're not going to keep you hidden, either. Tomorrow we'll go walking in town, and I just dare Dr. Dredd to try anything."

"But I'm afraid. . . ."

"Don't be afraid, Calvin. That's what Dr. Dredd wants. If you stand up to him, you'll be safe. Mama and me and . . . and all the people of Coven Tree will see to that."

"I . . . I'll stay the night," said Calvin. "For I am dead tired after the rainmaking and running away and all. But tomorrow I'll have to make plans of how to stay out of Dredd's clutches. I believe you two women just don't understand what kind of a creature Dr. Dredd is. Not you, Mrs. McCabe, nor you either, Ellen. You just don't understand."

Still later that same evening, Ellen sat alone in the living room, waving a palm-leaf fan to make a small breeze in the still, hot air.

From the next room came the sound of her mother

clumping down the stairs. "I put Calvin in the attic room," said Mrs. McCabe. "And loaned him one of your pa's nightshirts. The poor boy was purely done in. He was asleep before his head hit the pillow."

"Mama?"

"Yes, Ellen?"

"D'you think Dr. Dredd's as terrible as Calvin made out?"

Mrs. McCabe sighed deeply and sank down onto the sofa. "Anyone who'd take a whip to another human being is purely evil, as I see it," she said. "But all those things Calvin told us—well, it'd take a creature more than human to do all that."

"Like Magda the Witch?"

"Oh, Magda's all right. She's even spoken kindly to me on occasion. But this Dr. Dredd's a different kind of creature altogether. The spawn of the Devil, if you ask me."

Ellen felt a little shiver go up her spine. "Do you think he'll come looking for Calvin?"

"I reckon he might. And before he does, we've got to—"

BOOM BOOM BOOM The pounding on the front door sounded like strokes of doom.

"Mama, you don't suppose . . ." Ellen started to get up.

"You stay where you are, young lady," her mother ordered. "With your father away, I'm head of this house."

Mrs. McCabe went to the door and opened it. Peering around her mother as she blocked the doorway, Ellen saw the outline of a gaunt man in a high, red hat. In his right hand he carried a whip of braided leather.

"Dr. Dredd—Dr. Hugo Dredd—at your service." Dredd's voice was as smooth as melted tar as he swept the hat from his head and made a low bow. "This is the McCabe house, I believe?"

"It is," answered Mrs. McCabe. "State your business, Dredd. It's an odd hour to be paying a call."

"True—true. But you see, I . . ." Dr. Dredd looked past Mrs. McCabe into the living room. "Wouldn't we all be more comfortable if I came inside?"

"I'm perfectly comfortable right here," said Mrs. McCabe, without budging an inch. "What's your business, sir?"

"You have something that belongs to me—my property, if you will. I want it back."

"What property, Dredd?"

"A boy, ma'am. Bufu, the Rainmaker, to be exact."

"A boy? Property?" Mrs. McCabe looked sternly at Dredd. "No one person can own another, Dr. Dredd."

"We quibble over mere words," said Dr. Dredd. "Call him my . . . my associate, if it pleases you. In any case, I want him—now! If you haven't seen him, perhaps your daughter . . ."

"As you can see, Dr. Dredd," said Ellen, feeling angry and frightened at the same time, "there's just us two ladies at home. So if you'll excuse us . . ."

"Perhaps then, I was mistaken." Dredd lifted his head and sniffed deeply through his beak of a nose. Then he looked down at Mrs. McCabe, and his face twisted into an awful scowl. "No, the boy's here, all right. Perhaps you know him as Bufu, or maybe he calls himself Calvin Huckabee. But he's in this house!"

"What makes you so all-fired sure of that?" snapped Mrs. McCabe.

"Wherever Calvin Huckabee goes," snarled Dredd, "the scent of rain and storm clouds hangs about him.

'Tis very faint, to be sure, and it takes a practiced nose to discover his whereabouts. But in our years of travel—and his few attempts to escape—I've learned to sniff him out as surely as the bloodhound follows the spoor of a fleeing fugitive."

"It's very late," said Mrs. McCabe in a voice that was deadly calm. "I think you'd better go now."

"The boy has a task which should begin tomorrow," replied Dredd. "Mayor Phipps and I have already concluded the bargain on it. So I *must have him*! Turn him over to me now and spare yourselves the calamity that my anger can bring down upon your heads!"

"Well, I never!" gasped Mrs. McCabe. "Mister, if you don't get out of my doorway this instant, I'll . . ."

With a hideous grin, Dredd waved a hand toward the end of the porch, where a green pillow in a rocking chair could be seen by the light from the window. "The pillow there—it's pretty, is it not?"

"It's pretty enough," said Mrs. McCabe. "I made it myself, and . . ."

Suddenly Dredd's right hand jerked back, then forward. The leather whip whirred through the air and . . .

WHAP

Where the pillow had been was a cloud of feathers. As they settled to the porch floor, Mrs. McCabe stared at the pillow's cover, now slit open as if by a keen knife.

"I want the boy!" thundered Dredd. "And I shall have him. Out of my way, madam!"

Mrs. McCabe moved back from the doorway, her eyes wide with fright. Dredd stepped into the living room. He took a second step . . . a third . . .

Then he stopped in midstride. "Wait!" he cried in a trembling voice. "Don't!"

Mrs. McCabe turned around to see what Dredd was staring at.

There in the kitchen doorway stood Ellen. Clutched in her arms was an old twin-barreled shotgun, pointed straight at Dredd.

"Drop that whip," Ellen commanded. "Drop it, I say!"

The whip thudded to the floor.

"Now leave this house! And don't forget to close the

door behind you."

Dredd's snarl was that of a mad dog. But he backed slowly out onto the porch. Mrs. McCabe sprang to the door, slammed it shut and threw the bolt home.

For a moment both Ellen and her mother stood in trembling silence. Mrs. McCabe breathed a loud sigh of relief.

"Well, if you ain't the plucky one, Ellen," she crowed. "But now you'd better put that gun back before it goes off accidental-like."

Ellen shook her head. "Dredd could come back."

"I doubt it. Looked to me like you scared him out of a year's growth. He'll know better the next—"

And then Ellen and her mother heard the awful laughing. It was evil and menacing, and it came from the darkness beyond the porch.

"Hear me, you wretched women. True, you've bested me—for now. But there'll be another time. Oh, you've not heard the last of Dr. Hugo Dredd and his Wagon of Wonders. No . . . no indeed!"

CHAPTER FOUR

Small Rain

The following morning Calvin trudged into the kitchen, rubbing his eyes and yawning. Ellen and her mother were just finishing their breakfast.

"I surely appreciate your mending and washing my clothes," said Calvin. "They look real nice now."

"Sit at the table, and I'll fix you a plate," said Mrs. McCabe.

"Yes'm. But I still don't think it's wise for me to stay in Coven Tree while Dr. Dredd's looking for me."

"Rubbish!" Ellen exclaimed. "Why, last night Dr. Dredd—"

Mrs. McCabe dropped a pot onto the stove with a loud clang and gave Ellen a look that would have fried eggs. "I think we've heard enough about Dr. Dredd," she said firmly. "Now both of you get a move on, or we'll be late for church."

"Church?" said Calvin in surprise. "I'm not going to any church."

"Why not?" Ellen asked. "It's Sunday, isn't it? On Sunday everybody in town goes to church."

"I'm not dressed for it. I ain't got no fancy clothes."

Mrs. McCabe looked him up and down. "You look presentable," she said. "Clean is all that's expected in church. No need to tog yourself out like some popinjay."

"You might douse your head under the pump in the yard," added Ellen. "It'll get the sleep out of your eyes and make your hair slick down. I'll lend you a comb when you're done."

Calvin stomped out through the back door, mumbling to himself.

As hard as he worked at the handle of the pump in

the yard, Calvin brought up only a trickle of greenish water to the spout. He cupped some in his hand and used it to scrub the rest of the dark stain from his face. Then he wiped himself dry on a sleeve of his shirt.

"That'll do," he whispered to his reflection in the bottom of the pump bucket. "And from here on, Mrs. McCabe, you and Ellen can just stop giving orders. 'Tain't a woman's place to treat a man like that."

As soon as he returned to the kitchen, Mrs. McCabe was at him again. "Tuck in your shirttail, Calvin."

"I don't have to . . ." But one look at Mrs. McCabe's firm jaw and steely eyes, and Calvin's resolve vanished. "Yes, ma'am."

On the way to church, Ellen started in. "Calvin, those long legs of yours are getting you too far ahead of us. Stop now, so we can catch up."

"Yes, ma'am."

"Don't call me ma'am, silly. I'm not a grown-up lady yet."

"Yes, ma'am . . . I mean Ellen."

Women and girls—Calvin didn't know as he'd ever get used to 'em.

* * *

When Calvin entered the church with Ellen and Mrs. McCabe, all heads turned to see the new boy in town. Even without the dark stain and costume someone must have recognized him from yesterday's show, because he heard the word *Bufu* whispered a few times.

Mrs. McCabe and Ellen sat on one of the benches with Calvin between them. He slouched way down. Having people sneak glances at him made him nervous.

"Sit up straight," Ellen whispered in his ear. "You ain't ashamed to be seen with Mama and me, are you?"

If Calvin even considered speaking up to Ellen, the way she looked at him changed his mind. "Yes, Ellen," he said meekly. "I mean, no, Ellen."

The old organ wheezed, and the choir began singing. All at once, Calvin felt protected—really safe and out of danger—for the first time since he'd run away. Dr. Dredd wouldn't pursue him here. He had always made Calvin keep away from such places. He didn't like 'em.

Reverend Terwilliger took as his text for the sermon the story of the prodigal son. As the tale unwound of the boy who got into all kinds of trouble after leaving home, Calvin wondered if he'd ever have a real home like the McCabes'.

After the service, it was the custom to gather in front of the church to exchange gossip. Naturally word about Bufu had spread, and just about everybody crowded about Calvin.

Mrs. McCabe introduced him, and then Ellen told about how he'd been mistreated by Dr. Dredd and had run away. Then, while Calvin's face turned as red as fire, she lifted his shirt to show the whip marks on his back.

"Why, that's an awful thing!" exclaimed Mamie Ross. "Who'd have thought that charming Dr. Dredd was such a mean person?"

"We ought to run him and his Wagon of Wonders clean out of town," added Eleanor Toofie.

There was a general murmur of agreement from the rest of the people.

Then Mayor Phipps spoke up. "If you folks feel that strong about getting rid of Dr. Dredd, I guess my deal with him to make rain is off," he announced.

"You made a deal with Dredd for rain?" asked Elijah Mason. "First we heard of it, Eli."

"Mebbe we shouldn't be too hasty in judging Dredd," someone else cried out. "Perhaps the boy deserved a beating. We don't want to upset the man who can bring us rain."

"That's right, Eli," called another voice. "Why should we chance missing our rain just for some lad who doesn't even live here?"

Ellen stomped her foot angrily. "Will you people listen to yourselves?" she demanded angrily. "Would you let a human being get treated worse'n an animal just to bring some water down from the sky? I never heard the like!"

But the single word *Rain!* was on everyone's lips. "We surely don't want Dr. Dredd backing out of the deal now," said Elijah Mason.

Calvin raised his hand for quiet. "You needn't worry about Dr. Dredd's backing off from his bargain," he said. "I've seen how he works, and if he made a deal, he'll try to hold you to it, come what may."

"Then why should we worry about your taking a licking or two?" called a voice.

"It's not me you should be worrying about, but yourselves," Calvin exclaimed. "For Dr. Dredd demands an awful price for any services he gives."

A confused murmuring came from the people about him. "Awful price?" muttered a woman. And "What's the lad talking about?" queried a voice from the rear.

"But Dredd can't make the rain himself," Calvin went on. "He can only force me to do it. And I'm not about to obey him anymore. But if you'll help me get away from him, I'll come back, once I'm truly free, and give you more rain than you'd see in a month of Sundays."

At that, the mood of the crowd changed once more. Dire threats against Dr. Dredd for daring to harm a fine boy like Calvin were shouted out loudly. Men and women gathered about him to shake his hand and pat him on the shoulder in friendly fashion.

"Good lad," said Mayor Phipps. "I'd rather deal with a youngster like you than with Dr. Dredd any day. I'll see he's sent packing, first thing tomorrow."

"I don't think it's going to be that easy," said Calvin.

"But I'll have the full power of the law behind me!"

"Begging your pardon, sir. But Dr. Dredd has powers of another kind."

At this, the mayor looked kind of puzzled. But then

he bustled off, full of his own importance.

At the same time, flighty Mrs. Benthorn from the big house up on the hill got Ellen off to one side. "A likely-looking boy, that Calvin," said Mrs. Benthorn, raising her eyebrows and fluttering the little fan she always carried. "Though he could use a little more meat on his bones. You'd best watch him well, Ellen McCabe."

"Why?" asked Ellen.

"There are lots of young ladies in Coven Tree who'd be interested in Calvin Huckabee. Very interested indeed. You've got him for now, but they'll take him away from you quicker'n scat if you're not careful."

Ellen could feel her face getting all hot and flushed. "D'you think me and Calvin . . ." she gasped. "That Calvin and me . . ."

"A word to the wise, dear, should be sufficient," cooed Mrs. Benthorn with another flutter of her fan. She turned about and paraded off down the street.

"Me? Soft on Calvin Huckabee?" Ellen cried, outraged. "Oh . . . pooh!" She stuck out her tongue at the retreating Mrs. Benthorn.

Ellen had planned on taking Calvin home after

church, but Mrs. McCabe would have none of it. "You show Calvin the village, Ellen," she said. "I'll have dinner on by the time you get back."

"But Mother!"

"Calvin's got to learn his way around Coven Tree sometime," said Mrs. McCabe firmly. "And he shouldn't do it alone. Not with Dredd around. You go along with him now."

That's how Calvin and Ellen found themselves on the dusty main street of Coven Tree, ambling toward the general store.

Right away, they got to arguing.

"Mrs. Benthorn thought you and me was sweet on each other, Calvin," said Ellen. "Did you ever hear anything so silly?"

"It sure is," Calvin replied. "There's no more chance of that happening than of a frog having kittens."

Ellen scowled at him. "And just what do you mean by that?" she asked crossly. "What's wrong with me?"

"Nothing. I was just agreeing with what you said."

"I'll have you know, there are a lot of boys who think I'm something really special."

"Well I'm not one of 'em, that's for sure."

"Of all the ill-mannered clods, you take first prize, Calvin Huckabee." Ellen pointed her nose high into the air.

"Now you don't have to go getting all uppity just because I . . . Oh!"

Calvin suddenly cried out in surprise as something leaped out at them from behind a corner of a building. At first it appeared to be a gigantic black bat. But then he saw it was an old woman in a black cape, with a pointed, wide-brimmed hat on her head. Her face was seamed with wrinkles, and a wart decorated the end of her long, curved nose. She stood before them in the middle of the road, waving her arms about.

"Who's that?" he asked in alarm.

"Just Old Magda," said Ellen, who couldn't help giggling. "She's the Coven Tree witch. But she doesn't scare me none."

"A witch?" Calvin said. "You don't suppose Dr. Dredd sent her to . . ."

"Old Magda won't harm you, you ninny. Folks say she's lived in these parts for more'n three hundred years. Time was, she could cast spells like nobody's business. But nowadays she's weak and old and spent. A lot of people laugh at her."

"Spoon of iron," chanted Old Magda as she moved slowly toward them, *"knife of lead. This be the son of Dr. Dredd!"*

"Now stop that, Old Magda!" ordered Ellen. "How'd you know about Calvin anyway? You wasn't in church."

"I knew of the coming of the Wagon of Wonders long before it arrived here," said the witch. "I can still foretell the future, you know. And Ellen, I mean to protect you from this wicked . . ."

"There's nothing wicked about Calvin. Just some bad manners, that's all. He's running away from Dr. Dredd."

"Running away?" asked Old Magda in surprise. "Drat! I failed to see that in the mystic design at the bottom of my teacup this morning. I'll have to brew up a new pot, soon as I get home." She patted Calvin on the shoulder with a knobby hand.

"So you've left Dredd, have you, lad?" she went on. "Good, good. But have a care, Calvin Huckabee. For Dredd is no mean enemy. Compared to his powers, the spells I had in the prime of my witchhood were as nothing."

"Oh!" cried Ellen, getting a bit frightened. "Is Dr. Dredd really that bad?"

"Bad?" croaked the witch. "Beings like Dredd sit at the right hand of Satan himself. From time to time he sends them here to earth to walk the land and bring ruin and chaos to all they meet. Mere mortals cannot recognize them for the evil creatures they are."

The witch winked one rheumy eye and tapped the side of her head. "But Old Magda knows. Yes, indeed."

"I think we've heard quite enough about Dr. Dredd for the present," said Ellen. "Old Magda, can't you say hello to Calvin?"

"Hello to Calvin," grumbled the witch.

"I . . . I'm mighty pleased to meet you, Miss Magda," Calvin replied.

"Miss Magda?" The witch honored Calvin with a toothless smile. "You were wrong about the lad, Ellen. He does indeed have good manners. Most folks jeer at me now, but he shows the proper respect for a witch. I'll walk along with you for a bit, if you don't mind."

"Well, I . . . I guess it'll be all right," said Ellen.

They continued toward the center of town, with Calvin in the middle, Ellen on one side of him and Old Magda on the other.

Say now, do you remember me—Stew Meat? I'm the one telling you this story. And here's where I come back into it. I saw for myself what happened next. It was astonishing, to say the least.

After church, some of the men in Coven Tree are in the habit of gathering in front of my store to discuss the affairs of the week. I've put a couple of benches there alongside the dirt road, and the wide front steps provide plenty of seats. It's a good place to talk about farming and politics and who owns the fastest horse in the county and how many angels can dance on the head of a pin.

On this particular Sunday I was there, of course. And Uncle Poot the dowser man, Sumner Beezum the jokester, Sheriff Houck, Arlo Denker and a number of others.

When Sumner Beezum spotted Old Magda coming his way, he couldn't resist the temptation to have a jest at her expense. He seemed to enjoy getting the witch riled up, now that she was too old and feeble to work a spell on him.

"Behold Old Magda, sirs!" he cried out. "I reckon I've seen prunes with fewer wrinkles on 'em."

Old Magda snarled once in Sumner's direction. But that was all.

Sumner tried again. "Why don't you conjure up a potion, old hag," he hooted, "one that'll make the boy there love you forever—warts and all?"

With that, Calvin stopped in his tracks and slowly turned to face Sumner. "You've got no call to talk to a lady that way," he told Sumner softly.

Old Magda clutched Ellen's arm, grinning with pleasure. "Calvin called me a lady!" she said, surprised. "First time I've been called that in . . . why, eighty or a hundred years."

Sumner now started in on Calvin. "What are you going to do, Bufu?" he sneered. "Soak me with rain?"

"I could," Calvin replied. " 'Tain't hard for anybody with half a brain to make it rain. But that don't include you, old man."

As you might guess, that's when everybody began laughing at Sumner. He got all red in the face, and I could tell he was thinking up some insult. Finally he flipped the cigar he'd been puffing on out into the dusty road at Calvin's feet. "Put that out with your pesky rain, young sharp-tongue," he said. "Else we may think you're a braggart as well as a mule-tongued lout."

That was mighty strong talk indeed. Calvin guided Ellen and Old Magda to the far side of the road. Then he stared across at Sumner.

"D'you think I can't?" Calvin asked.

"Well . . . perhaps you can," said Sumner, probably remembering the storm of yesterday. "But it'd be a shame to get my Sunday suit all soaked."

"I figured you'd back down, old man," said Calvin. "So I'll just make rain enough to douse the cigar. We'll all remain dry."

"That's impossible!" Sumner hooted.

"And if I did it—would you then agree that you're just a silly old windbag?"

"Calvin Huckabee!" snapped Ellen. "You're going too far. You've got no call to . . ."

"Let the lad go on!" urged Old Magda. "Let him go on!"

Sumner Beezum chuckled loudly. "So you're going to make it rain on the cigar, but none of us will get wet in the slightest. What kind of folderol is this, boy?"

"I can do it," declared Calvin.

That's when all of us men began laughing. All except Uncle Poot the dowser man. "Careful, Sumner," said Uncle Poot. "Water is my business. The lad has the smell of storms and wet weather about him. I believe he can do it."

"Poppycock!" replied Sumner. "But he's welcome to try if he wishes. It'll be fun, seeing him make a fool of himself."

"And if I succeed," said Calvin to Sumner, "will you stop teasing Old Magda?"

At that, Sumner Beezum found himself backed into a corner. He couldn't refuse without admitting Calvin's power. "I . . . I'll leave her be," he mumbled.

Magda cackled triumphantly, but Ellen looked worried. "Can you really do it?" she whispered to Calvin. "It wouldn't do to become a laughingstock your first day in Coven Tree."

"Oh, I can do it all right," he replied. "But you're not to start fretting when I start in."

"Why would I do that?"

"Every time I make it rain, my head gets to hurting and pounding. But this-here rain will be so small, the pain won't amount to much."

With that, Calvin set to work. He sank down onto his knees and put his hands on either side of his head. His eyes closed, and his face got all twisty. Little moans came from his throat.

"Small . . . rain . . ." I heard him mutter. Then the moaning began again.

For a minute by my watch we stood there watching Calvin turn his body this way and that, with the sun beating down on his back. Suddenly Uncle Poot gave a little cry.

"Look," he said, pointing.

In the air above the road a tiny cloud had appeared, no higher than the roof of the store. It was right above the smoldering cigar.

The top of the cloud billowed upward while the bottom got blacker and blacker. We all heard a wee clap of thunder, little louder than a sneeze. The cloud was the same shape as the huge thunderheads I'd seen in years past above Coven Tree just before a storm.

But this one was no larger than a barrel of molasses.

SPUTT

The first raindrop hit the road, quickly soaking into the dust.

SPUTT SPUTT

Two more drops fell. Then, right before our eyes, the rain began in earnest, slashing down onto the roadway in sheet after sheet of wetness.

The cigar hissed loudly . . . and then winked out.

There were cries of astonishment among the men in front of my store as they stared at the soggy cigar and the little circle of damp soil that surrounded it. Calvin Huckabee got to his feet. He was still grasping his head in his hands.

"Calvin, are you all right?" Ellen touched his cheek lightly with the tips of her fingers.

"I'll be just fine in a little while," he replied. "But it was real kind of you to ask."

"Why don't you kiss the lad and have done with it?" cried Old Magda.

Ellen snatched her hand away like she'd burnt her fingers.

Above us, the cloud was caught by a passing breeze

and whipped away. But for the wet spot in the road, nobody would have known the miniature thunderstorm had ever happened.

"Now then, Sumner Beezum!" screeched Old Magda. "Next time you see me, I'm to be treated with a bit more respect. Understand? Otherwise the whole town will know you're not a man of your word."

Then the witch turned to Calvin. "From now on, I'm your friend, Calvin Huckabee," she told him. "I hope one day to return the kindness you've shown me."

With that, she started off toward the forest at the edge of town. "I must go home now and feed my owl, Hecate," she called back. "Come see me, Calvin, whenever you need me."

"I'll do that," Calvin answered. "But Dr. Dredd . . ."

"I'm getting sick of hearing about Dr. Dredd," said Ellen. "It won't be long before he gives up on you and goes his way. After all, what can he do against the whole of Coven Tree?"

In the clearing at the edge of town, a single light glimmered in the windows of Dr. Dredd's Wagon of Wonders. Inside the wagon Dredd had cleared one of the tables. On it lay Antaeus. The wrestler's body now seemed no larger than that of an average man.

Dredd poured oil into his palm from a small bottle. He spread the oil on Antaeus's shoulders.

"I found you, O mighty Antaeus, in your tomb far away, covered with the dust of antiquity," Dredd chanted. "And I gave you new life so that you might again astound mankind with your great strength. Now, you will do my bidding."

"Do . . . your . . . bidding," rumbled Antaeus.

"You must recover the boy and return him to my Wagon of Wonders. Only when he has brought rain can I complete the spell I've begun to cast over the people of Coven Tree."

"Return . . . boy. . . ."

"You, Antaeus, are the son of Terra, from whom your great strength comes. Compared to you, the power of mere mortals is like that of a newborn child. Never, except at the hands of Hercules, did you know defeat."

"Never . . . know . . . defeat. . . ."

"So we will seek out Calvin Huckabee. And you will fight with whoever presumes to stand in our way. To the death, if necessary."

"To . . . the . . . death . . ." came the deep reply. "I . . . go . . . now. . . ."

"Not yet." Dr. Dredd looked up and down the length of the wagon. The displays had been safely locked away, and only the armor of the mysterious Black Knight of Etherium glittered in the dim light.

"Today is the Sabbath. On the Sabbath, my powers—and yours—are at their weakest. But tomorrow—tomorrow we will do what must be done."

"Tomorrow. . . ."

CHAPTER FIVE

No Holds Barred

The next morning—Monday—Ellen was standing at the mirror, getting herself ready for school, while Mrs. McCabe dumped chunks of wood into the box beside the stove. Calvin was still up in the attic, asleep.

"Land sakes!" Ellen exclaimed. "Calvin's doing enough sleeping for three people. I wish I had nothing better to do than loll around in bed all day."

"He needs his rest," Mrs. McCabe replied. "I have no doubt he got little enough of it while he was in

Dredd's hands. And while he's sleeping, we have to talk, young lady."

"Talk? About what?"

"About Calvin. And the way you've been treating him."

"Me? Why, didn't I bring him in from the shed and see he got fed and mend his clothes and . . ."

"Yes," said her mother. "And ever since then you've been ordering him around like he was nothing but a puppy dog and you were its master. It's been 'Calvin, stand up straight,' and 'Calvin, don't slurp your soup,' and Calvin this and Calvin that. You pick at that boy worse than as if you were married to him."

"But Mama, he's such a . . . a lout. And besides, I've heard you doing the same thing."

"Not like you, Ellen. All last evening, while you were telling me about the rain he'd made, he couldn't make a move or say a word but you were jawing at him."

"How else am I going to learn him . . . teach him . . . any kind of manners?"

"You're not going to turn somebody with an up-bringing like he's had into a fine gentleman over-night," said Mrs. McCabe. "Besides, what do you care how he acts? He'll be moving on, just as soon as Dr. Dredd's been scotched. We'll never see him again after that, more'n likely."

Ellen was shocked at the idea. "Mama, do you really think he'd go off and . . ."

"We've got no claim on him, Ellen. So don't look so surprised. D'you know who you remind me of?"

"Who?"

"Me, that's who. When your pa was courting me, I used to order him about something fierce. That way, I figured folks wouldn't know we was sweet on one another."

Ellen looked at her mother peevishly. "You're beginning to sound just like Mrs. Benthorn," she said. "She thought I'd taken a liking to Calvin, too."

"Have you, Ellen?"

"Have I what?"

"Have you got more interest in Calvin Huckabee than just helping him get away from Dr. Dredd?"

"Ohhh . . . Mama!" Ellen grabbed her comb and yanked it hard through her long brown hair. "Sometimes you make me wish I was born an orphan!"

* * *

It was nearly an hour later, and Ellen had long since set off for school, when Calvin plodded downstairs. "Sit yourself down and have breakfast," said Mrs. McCabe. "After that, I've got a list of chores as long as my arm. You're not afraid of honest work, are you?"

"No, ma'am," replied Calvin. "But I do think it'd be better if I was moving on, Mrs. McCabe."

"Move on? Today?" asked Mrs. McCabe. "Having you here is no trouble, Calvin, and I can use your help around the place. Besides, here you're safe from Dr. Dredd."

"Safe?" replied Calvin. "I don't think anybody's safe as long as he's about."

"But the whole village . . ."

"There have been other villages, ma'am. I've seen 'em. And it hasn't been pretty."

Mrs. McCabe eyed him curiously and then sat down at the table. "What do you mean, 'other villages,' Calvin?" she asked.

"Well, there was Mapleton down in New Hampshire, and Halpinsburgh and Busby Corners. . . . It's always the same."

"The same, Calvin? I don't understand."

"Dr. Dredd comes into a new town, where the people are all happy and kind to one another and pleased with the way they're living. Then everybody goes through the Wagon of Wonders. After that, Dr. Dredd makes a deal for something the village thinks it needs."

"A deal?"

"Yes'm. Once it was for somebody to lick the town bully. Antaeus took care of that, right quick. Another time, fifteen acres of hardwood needed cutting for a railroad spur. It'd take a team of men months to do it, but Dredd got it finished overnight, though I don't know how. But afterward . . ."

"What happens afterward, Calvin?" asked Mrs. McCabe.

"The place begins to change. Everybody seems to forget about being decent to one another. Instead, they're all wrapped up in their own wants and desires, and nothing'll do but to get ahead of the next person. If that takes lying and cheating or even fighting, so be it."

"A thing like that could *never* happen in Coven Tree," declared Mrs. McCabe.

"Yes it could," said Calvin. "Sometimes we'd hear about it from other travelers along the road. Or else Dr. Dredd would go back to a place where he'd put on a show months before. It was always the same. Buildings falling to ruin for lack of proper care, and the animals weak from not being fed and weeds growing in the fields. Men and women all snarling at one another and even fighting right in the streets. It was like all those fine people had been changed into a pack of mad dogs."

"That . . . that's horrible, Calvin," gasped Mrs. McCabe.

"It is," agreed Calvin. "But the most horrible thing was Dredd himself. He'd look about at all that destruction and he'd . . . he'd laugh. 'See, Calvin,' he'd cry out. 'See what I've done for this charming little town!' "

"Dr. Dredd could do all that . . . by himself?" asked Mrs. McCabe, stunned.

"It happens every time."

"Well, it won't happen here," declared Mrs. McCabe. "We'll be ready for Dr. Dredd, whenever he appears."

"It won't make no difference. Once the bargain's made and Dr. Dredd carries out his part, you'll be in his power."

"But Coven Tree needs rain. And you, Calvin . . ." Suddenly Mrs. McCabe grew ominously silent.

"You finally understand, don't you?" said Calvin. "Dr. Dredd needs me to work his spell this time. That's why he'll be after me. And he'll use whatever it takes to get me back."

"But the village . . ."

Calvin shook his head. "The village can't hold out against Dr. Dredd. I know. The only way I can think of to save you is for me to move on. Mebbe by the time he catches me, I'll be so far away he'll think twice about returning here."

"No, Calvin," said Mrs. McCabe. "Despite how much they're longing for rain, the people of Coven Tree have too much self-respect to grovel before Dr. Dredd's magic and evil spells. They just need time to think things over, that's all. This village has held out against freeze and drought and hail and flood and witches and demons and the Devil himself. We've seen them all, yet we've endured. And we'll do it again."

Calvin kind of smiled. "I never seen anybody so set in their ways as you are," he said. "Perhaps you people can defeat Dr. Dredd after all. But wouldn't it be better if I was to go off somewhere and hide?"

"You'll do nothing of the kind, Calvin Huckabee. You'll walk the streets of Coven Tree, and you'll walk proud. Whatever Dredd had in mind, he'll not be able to say he won because we were afraid."

"Yes, ma'am," replied Calvin doubtfully.

By the middle of the afternoon, Calvin had mended a squeaky stair tread, fashioned a new handle for the grain shovel and fixed a broken harness in the barn. Mrs. McCabe had plenty of other chores for him, though.

"There's some big rocks that boiled up in the vegetable garden over the winter," she said. "Hitch up the horse and see if they can be dragged off somewhere. The horse's name is Delilah, and she won't give you no trouble unless you take a stick to her."

"If Delilah's the horse in the near stall in the barn, she shouldn't be doing no pulling," said Calvin.

"Why not? She's healthy and willing."

"Yes, ma'am. But she's thrown one of her shoes.

While I was fixing the harness, I saw her kind of favoring one leg in her stall. She shouldn't be worked with only three shoes on."

"Course not. Tell you what—you take her to Sven Hensen's smithy in town and have her shod. It shouldn't take long. You'll have plenty of time afterward to haul rocks."

"Yes, ma'am."

So along about three o'clock, Calvin found himself in the center of town, heading for the blacksmith shop. The first thing he saw as he reached the door was Sven Hensen, standing at his anvil and repairing a busted plow point.

Sven's the biggest man in Coven Tree. And the strongest. Over six feet tall, he's got a chest like a boulder and arms and legs bigger around than many men's waists. Sven's usually a calm and placid man, and I never saw him get riled but once. That was when Randell Dibbs and his five grown sons made some remarks during prayer meeting that Sven didn't consider seemly. He went over to where they was sitting, picked up two of the boys—one under each arm—and tossed them out onto the street. As you might imagine, Randell didn't like that one bit. When Sven came back for a second load, Randell and his oldest son leaped onto Sven's back and began pounding him with their fists. Sven carried them—and the other two sons under his arms—outside with no more trouble than as if he'd been toting pillows. The Dibbs boys and their pa haven't been back to prayer meeting since.

Sven spotted Calvin in the doorway, holding Delilah's bridle rein. "You da new boy who stay at McCabe house, huh?" said the blacksmith. "An' ol' Delilah need a new shoe. You bring her right inside. I be vit' you, soon as I finish here."

Calvin went in. Delilah's hoofs clip-clopped on the smithy's hard-packed earth floor. Sven continued pounding the metal of the plow point. Then, all at once the inside of the shop seemed to grow darker. Both Calvin and the blacksmith looked toward the entrance.

In the doorway stood Dr. Dredd. Behind him, looming up like a mountain, was Antaeus. In Dredd's eyes was an unearthly light, like the glowing coals of the forge.

"Yah? Vat you want, you two?" asked Sven. "Vhatever it is, you gonna have to vait. I got plow to do, an' den . . ."

"Keep to your work, blacksmith," said Dredd. "I came to fetch my boy back, that's all."

"No!" cried Calvin. "I'm not going . . ."

"But you are," replied Dredd. "You may walk if you'd care to. If not, Antaeus can carry you."

"If boy don't vanno go, he ain't gotta go," said Sven. He plunged the plow point into a tub of water, where it boiled and sizzled.

"This is none of your business," snapped Dredd.

"Den I make it my business," replied Sven. He reached behind him and grasped a thick hickory rod that was leaning against the forge.

"Antaeus!" Dredd waved a finger at the wrestler and then pointed at Sven. "Go!"

With amazing speed, Antaeus sprang at the blacksmith. Quick as a striking snake he snatched the rod from Sven's hand. Calvin thought the wrestler was going to strike Sven. Instead, Antaeus broke the rod across one knee as easily as if it had been a dry twig instead of a massive club nearly as strong as steel.

"Antaeus, take the boy," Dredd ordered. "If we hurry, he'll have rain falling within the hour."

"Joost you vait, mister," said Sven, scowling at Dredd. "Ain't nobody gonna take dis boy avay unless he vanna go. Dis my place, not yours."

"Oh?" said Dredd calmly. "And are you going to prevent it?"

"You betcha I am. An' I'm not scared of your friend there, neither."

"Really?" A smile like a toothy grave spread across Dredd's face. "Do you wish to fight him for the boy?"

"I fight him—or you—or the Devil himself to keep peace in my shop," declared Sven. "Don't nobody get dragged out of here unless I do the dragging."

"Then if there's to be a fight, perhaps we should go outside," said Dredd. "It's a bit cramped in here."

With that, Dredd led Antaeus out into the sunlight. Sven followed, leaving Calvin standing fearfully in the doorway.

Sven stripped off his shirt and stood facing Antaeus. "Are ve gonna have dis a reg'lar wrestling match?" Sven asked.

Dredd shook his head. "Antaeus knows little of the

niceties of the sport," he said. "He prefers no-holds-barred."

Sven wiped his forehead with the back of one arm. No-holds-barred wrestling had no rules. Gouging, kicking, using whatever weapons came to hand—all were allowed. A man could be hurt—perhaps seriously.

From the porch of my store I saw the two gigantic men preparing to fight. This was something I didn't want to miss. I put up my CLOSED sign on the front door and trotted to the edge of the smithy's big front yard. A few other villagers had collected there, and more were coming all the time.

"Do you wish to withdraw," Dredd asked of the blacksmith, "and let me take the boy in peace?"

"Nope." Sven shook his head. "I vin vit' any rules you name."

"Then let us begin." Dredd stepped aside, and the fight was on.

Sven trotted backward some twenty feet. He lowered his head. Then he came charging toward Antaeus like a runaway express train.

BOOM Sven's head slammed against Antaeus's chest,

and the sound was like a big bass drum being struck.

But unlike in the fight with Packer Vickery, this time Antaeus was braced and ready. He didn't even flinch. He stood as if rooted to the ground. It was Sven who bounced away, clutching his head.

Antaeus reached out, grasping Sven under one arm and the opposite leg. He lifted the blacksmith high over his head and slammed him to the ground.

Before Sven could recover, Antaeus was on him. One thick forearm pressed against the blacksmith's throat. Gurgling, choking sounds came from Sven's mouth.

"Stop it!" cried Calvin from the doorway. "You're strangling him!"

Antaeus paid Calvin no mind. He continued pressing down and shutting off Sven's wind. In desperation Calvin looked about and finally seized a lump of coal from the smithy floor. He hurled it at Antaeus as hard as he could.

The lump of coal, as big as a man's fist, struck Antaeus behind one ear. The wrestler looked about in surprise and finally spotted Calvin.

"Stop it!" Calvin shouted again.

Ponderously Antaeus got to his feet. On the ground, Sven began gulping in great breaths of air.

The crowd, which was getting bigger every moment, saw Antaeus lurch toward Calvin. Calvin looked to the right and the left. If he moved either way, Antaeus would be on him in an instant. And if he went backward—into the smithy—he'd be trapped.

That was what Ellen McCabe saw as she came around the bend in the road on her way home from school.

"Calvin!" she cried out as the monstrous wrestler came nearer to the boy. "No!"

Dropping her schoolbooks, she raced forward with her long skirt whipping about her legs. Just as Antaeus reached out to grasp Calvin, she threw herself upon the massive back.

She wrapped one arm about the huge neck. "Calvin, run!" she screamed.

Then she sank her teeth into Antaeus's ear.

"*Aaarrgh!*" Antaeus's cry of surprise and pain rang from the distant hills. He turned about. Of course Ellen, riding upon his back, turned with him. He blinked his small, piggy eyes, reached up, and tore Ellen's arm from about his neck. She fell from her slippery perch and tumbled to the ground.

Antaeus whirled around. Seeing Ellen lying before him, he raised one huge foot, preparing to stomp her like an ant.

THUMP Sven Hensen, forgotten when Calvin had thrown the coal, slammed into Antaeus's side, sending the wrestler spinning head over heels into the dirt.

"That'll fix him!" shouted one of the onlookers gleefully.

But it didn't. Antaeus got to his feet and looked around. He spotted a young oak tree near the smithy. Its trunk was nearly four inches across, and it was rooted deep in the ground. "Club!" he rumbled. "Need . . . club!" He grasped the trunk of the oak, twisting and pulling at the same time.

All of us watchers thought it was silly, of course. Nobody could possibly pull that tree out of the . . .

SNAP Deep within the earth, the tree's taproot parted. With a crackling sound, other roots gave way. The earth around the tree bulged and split as Antaeus lifted upward.

He pulled the tree from the ground like a tooth from its socket. Then he snapped off branches like they were dry twigs until all that remained was a huge club, eight feet long, with a ball of roots at its end. He swung the club with a loud *SWOOSH* and began striding toward Sven.

Ellen got to her feet and stood beside Calvin at the smithy door. "There's got to be some way to stop that big ox!" she cried. "Do something, Calvin."

"There's nothing *to* do," Calvin answered. "Nobody ever licked Antaeus. He's just too big and too strong."

SWOOSH Antaeus swung the club again, coming nearer and nearer the cowering blacksmith.

"But at the show . . . when he was standing on the platform . . ." Ellen gasped. "He didn't seem no bigger'n an ordinary man."

"That's because he didn't have his feet touching the ground," said Calvin. "Dr. Dredd says he gets his power from the earth. When he leaves it, he loses his strength. But where they're fighting, there's nothing *except* earth."

SWOOSH the huge club flashed by only inches from Sven's head.

Ellen ran forward toward the groggy blacksmith. "Sven!" she yelled. "Lift Antaeus off the ground! It's your only chance!"

Sven shook his head as if trying to clear it. Ellen didn't know whether he'd heard her or not. And if he did hear, would he listen? . . .

SWOOSH This time the roots at the end of the club made gashes along Sven Hensen's ribs.

But then, while the club was at the end of its swing, Sven lowered his head, rushed under his opponent's arms and clasped him around the waist. With a mighty heave the blacksmith lifted Antaeus clear off the ground.

For a moment the two fighters were still, like a living statue. Antaeus stretched out his feet, trying to touch the earth with his toes. Sven, gasping for breath, lifted him higher.

Suddenly the massive club dropped heavily to the ground. Antaeus went limp in Sven's arms.

Those of us who were watching murmured in wonder and astonishment. Antaeus was shrinking in the blacksmith's grasp. From the wrestler's mouth came loud groans of pain.

"Enough!" he cried. "No . . . more . . . fight!"

"You sure of dat?" demanded Sven, squeezing Antaeus even harder.

"No . . . more . . . fight!"

Sven dropped his opponent to the ground. Antaeus lay at the blacksmith's feet. But this time he didn't grow larger. Defeat seemed to have robbed him of his power.

After a single glance at his fallen champion, Dredd turned and scuttled toward the nearby woods.

"Antaeus . . . defeated!" he cried out. "Then so be it. The foolish beast is now condemned to wander the land as a half-witted mortal, weak and afraid, until he finds another like me to restore his powers. And that may be never. I have done with him!"

"Now, Dr. Dredd, it gonna be your turn!" roared Sven.

"I think not, blacksmith," Dredd answered with a grim smile. "I'll have the boy yet. In my wagon I have other treats in store. I'm not through with Coven Tree."

With that, Dredd darted in among the trees and was gone.

Later that day, Sheriff Houck and a band of deputies

went to the clearing west of town where Dredd's wagon had been. But it too had disappeared.

In the little house at the edge of town, Ellen, Mrs. McCabe and Calvin Huckabee sat up all night, waiting for they knew not what.

Deep within the swampy glade known as Fletcher's Bog, a single glimmer of light came from a window of Dr. Dredd's Wagon of Wonders. Dr. Dredd peered inside a large cupboard, looked long and hard at the dragon's black egg and passed talonlike fingers over its warm, rocklike surface. He shook his head.

Then he walked to one end of the wagon and grasped the helmet and chest plate of the Black Knight of Etherium. He dragged them the length of the wagon to where the leg pieces lay and fitted and hooked the armor together until it was whole.

Next he reached into a dark corner and drew forth a sword, long and heavy, that reflected the lantern light from edges as keen as razors.

"Now you are whole once more, oh great knight," Dredd chanted. "Gather your strength for what is to come. To those who know not your secret, you are invincible. Tomorrow you will descend on Coven Tree like the angel of death itself."

Dredd chuckled evilly and wiped a bit of dust from the helmet with his sleeve. Then he listened to a sound that started softly but soon became loud enough to drown out the croaking of the bullfrogs in the bog.

From somewhere deep within the armor came a low, hideous moaning.

CHAPTER SIX

Help from Old Magda

Nothing unusual occurred within the village that night. The next morning, though, we soon found out Dr. Dredd had been hard at work.

Sheriff Roscoe Houck came into my store about ten o'clock. He was the first person I'd seen all morning. With Dr. Dredd out there in the woods somewhere, folks seemed to be sticking pretty close to home.

"Morning, Stew Meat," said the sheriff. "Mighty odd doings outside of town last night. Did you hear?"

I shook my head. "How do you mean, odd?" I asked.

"Just east of here, there's mebbe a two- or three-hundred-foot stretch of the road where big trees are lying across it. A man on foot would have a hard time getting through, and a horse would never make it. It'll take a few days before we can clear it."

"Then I guess folks won't be going east for a little while," I said, trying to smile. But a strange shiver went up my backbone.

"No, nor west either," said Roscoe. "Seems there was a rock slide, and it's blocking the road and the railway too. Just at that cut through the mountains. Some of those boulders are nearly as big as a house."

By now I was feeling real uneasy. "Maybe you'd best tell Mayor Phipps to get down to the train station and send a wire to the governor's office. They can send help."

"We can't do that," said Roscoe with a shrug. "Telegraph lines are down. Somewhere out there in the woods. And I shudder to think what would happen to anybody we sent to fix 'em."

"What you're telling me, Roscoe," I said slowly, trying to keep my hands from trembling, "is that Coven Tree has been cut off from the rest of the world. We're all by ourselves here."

"Looks that way," the sheriff replied ominously. "Even if we sent a man on foot to get word out, it'd take some time."

"I don't think Dr. Dredd is going to allow any messages out," I said. "Things like this don't just happen. Unless somebody makes 'em happen, that is."

Roscoe nodded. "Mayor Phipps and I figured as much. But I don't want people getting all excited until we can figure out what to do. Right now, you're to come over to the mayor's office."

"What for?"

"Kind of a planning session. You're to be there, as you helped make the original deal for rain with Dredd. Me and the mayor, of course. Calvin Huckabee, for he's the cause of the whole thing. And Ellen McCabe."

"Ellen? What's she got to do with . . ."

"When I told Calvin about the meeting, Ellen insisted on coming along too. I tried to say no. But Calvin said that after Ellen had been brave enough to tackle Antaeus just to help him, she had a right to be in on any decisions that were being made. So what could I do?"

"I reckon it won't do no harm. I'll be there, Roscoe."

"Oh, and Stew Meat?"

"What?"

"Gimme the rest of those black jelly beans from the jar there. If we're in for a siege, I don't want to go through it without my supply of licorice jelly beans."

There were five of us in the mayor's office when Eli Phipps closed and locked the door. Five more frightened people you never saw in your life.

"I guess we'll have to figure on Dr. Dredd's returning to Coven Tree," the mayor began.

"Oh, he'll be back, sure as shooting," said Calvin. "Probably as soon as it gets dark. That's when his power seems to be the strongest. And he'll be madder'n ever, on account of Antaeus getting licked in the fight."

"The question is, Eli," I put in, "what are we going to do when he gets here?"

"I can get maybe five deputies together," said the sheriff, chewing a mouthful of jelly beans. "But if that

Dredd is as almighty as Calvin says, five men won't make much of a difference."

The mayor leaned back in his chair, staring at the ceiling. He seemed such a little man to be sitting in such a big chair. "I don't suppose," he said, and his voice was hoarse and raspy, "that we could cancel the deal we made for rain and just give Calvin back. . . ."

"No!" Ellen cried out. She grasped Calvin's arms. "You can't!"

"I certainly can!" Eli snapped. "As mayor of this town, I . . ."

"Now just hold on," I said. "Giving up Calvin won't help. You and I made a bargain with Dredd, Eli, and now he intends to hold us to it, no matter what. It won't do for us to lose our nerve at this time and start acting like cowards."

"And besides . . ." Ellen began.

"Will you be silent, child?" snapped the mayor.

"No, I won't be silent!" Ellen wrinkled her face at the word child. "Sheriff Houck is right. Five men wouldn't make much of a difference against Dredd's power."

"Ellen, we've already discussed . . ."

"But what if Dr. Dredd got here to find he was facing everybody in Coven Tree?"

"What?" cried Eli and Roscoe and me, all at the same time.

"Sure," said Ellen excitedly. "There must be near six hundred people in Coven Tree, if we count the farmers nearby. I bet Dr. Dredd would think twice before taking on a crowd like that."

"But there are women and children . . ." sputtered Eli.

"The children can stay locked snug inside their homes," said Ellen. "As for the women—well, we can fight as good as any men. You'll see."

"I . . . I dunno," mumbled Eli. "What do you think, Stew Meat?"

"It sounds like the only chance we've got," I said. "Maybe we'll win, and maybe we'll lose. But in any case, Dr. Dredd will know he's been in a fight."

I turned to Calvin. "What about it?" I asked. "You know Dredd better'n anybody here. Can we lick him?"

Calvin thought about this for a long time. "I've never seen Dr. Dredd bested, no matter what the odds," he said finally. "He has powers that are as strong as they are unholy. You'll be in for a peck of trouble."

Then he glanced at Ellen and kind of smiled. "But I guess you let yourselves in for trouble the minute you began helping me get free of Dredd."

"We can do it, Calvin," said Ellen. "We surely can!"

"Perhaps," said Calvin. "This here's the first town I've seen where the people would lift a finger to help me. Mebbe that'll make a difference. But if we lose, heaven help us all!"

"We won't lose," said Ellen. "You'll see, Calvin."

So the plan was made. Sheriff Houck and his men would notify all the villagers and outlying farmers to gather in town just before sunset. We counted on maybe three or four hundred showing up, bringing any kind of weapons they could lay their hands on. Beyond that, we had no real plan of battle. Who knew what Dr. Dredd would try?

Once outside the mayor's office, Ellen scurried along the village's dirt road with Calvin trotting alongside to keep up. "Where are you headed in such an all-fired hurry?" he asked.

"To Old Magda's," Ellen replied. "Maybe she can help somehow."

"By doing what?" asked Calvin mournfully.

"Who knows? After all, she is a witch. And we need all the help we can get."

Old Magda's house, down by Great Bog, was made of tree limbs and mud. Smoke drifted upward from a chimney of baked clay. Ellen knocked timidly at the door.

"Go away!" cried the witch's cracked voice from within. "I'm cooking a stew of lizard tails, and I don't want to be disturbed."

"You didn't tell Calvin Huckabee to go away when he helped you in town the other day," called Ellen.

"Calvin? You don't sound like Calvin."

"It's me, Miss Magda," said Calvin. "Ellen came along to . . . to show me the way."

Suddenly the door burst open, and the old crone peered out of the darkness within the tiny cottage. "Calvin, lad," she croaked. "Come in. Come in."

Ellen started forward.

"Wouldn't you like to remain outside, Ellen," asked

the witch sharply, "while Calvin and I have our little talk?"

"Old Magda, you have no manners at all!" With a toss of her head, Ellen marched into the cottage and sat in a chair made from an old barrel. She looked up at an owl, almost as ragged as Old Magda herself, that perched on a bookcase full of dusty volumes. The owl hooted.

"Quiet, Hecate!" commanded the witch. "That's no way to talk to our fine guest." Then she honored Calvin with a gap-toothed smile. "What can I do for you, lad?" she cooed.

"It—it's about Dr. Dredd," Calvin began. "We'd like to know what he's planning next, if . . . if you please, ma'am."

"Still afraid of Dr. Dredd, eh?" said the witch. "Oh, how I'd like to foil just one of his schemes. Now, let me see . . . let me see . . ."

She ran a bony finger along a shelf on one wall and finally drew forth a glass jar. "Let's see what the tea leaves have to say."

From a bucket she took a dipperful of brackish water

and poured it into a tiny cracked cup. Next, she dropped a pinch of tea leaves from the jar and watched them settle to the bottom.

"Shouldn't the tea water be hot, Old Magda?" asked Ellen.

"If water's hot, the fortune's rot," replied Old Magda in a singsong chant. *"But with cold brew, the fortune's true.* You leave witchcraft to those of us who understand it, girl."

"Yes'm," replied Ellen, trying to hide her annoyance.

Old Magda raised the cup to her mouth and sucked out as much water as she could. Then she ran to the window and spat it out. "Horrible-tasting stuff," she told Calvin. "If not for this awful drought I wouldn't have it in the house."

Closing one eye, she looked fixedly with the other at the pattern of tea leaves resting on the cup's bottom.

"I tell you that— That— Oh, drat!"

"What's the matter?" Calvin asked.

"These leaves only tell about the past. You both had scrambled eggs for breakfast yesterday, didn't you?

For the future, I need another jar. Only three hundred years old, and already I'm becoming absentminded. Drat again!"

She rinsed out the cup in the same bucket from which she'd dipped the water. Then she found another jar on the shelf. Opening it, she reached inside, removed something that appeared to be a ball of dust, and tossed it to the floor.

"Dead spider," she explained. "I warned the little scamp not to crawl in there while my back was turned."

She made a second cup of cold tea and drained off the water as she'd done before. Then she looked darkly into the cup.

"You, Calvin Huckabee," she chanted slowly, "will marry a circus bareback rider. Your children—twelve in all—will have six toes on each foot. You will make your living by selling bicycle chains and rat traps. Later on . . . Oh, no! That's not right, either!"

"What's the matter now?" asked Ellen with a sigh.

"The bottom of the cup is chipped," said Old Magda. "I was reading the chips as if they were tea leaves. Fetch me that magnifier, Calvin."

Calvin handed the witch a thick lens from the table.

As Old Magda held it to her face, one blinking eye seemed enormous. The gigantic eyeball stared down into the cup.

"I see danger ahead for the two of you," Old Magda muttered. "Yes, I've got it right this time. A creature black as night is being prepared. This creature carries in its hand a thing that gleams and brings utter destruction."

"Oh, dear!" cried Ellen. "Are you sure . . . ?"

"Absolutely," said Old Magda. "And I see the presence of Dr. Hugo Dredd over all. But wait!"

"What?" said Calvin. "What else do you see?"

"The dark creature has a secret. The secret of its own downfall. But . . ."

"But what?" Ellen demanded. "Tell us, Old Magda."

"But the secret will not be discovered until *after* the black creature is defeated."

"But that's no help at all," wailed Ellen. "Can't you at least tell us if we'll be the ones to defeat it? Or will it win . . . ?"

"I cannot tell. That part of the future is hidden. But perhaps—yes, wait a bit. Ah, there it is."

"There what is?" Calvin asked.

"Why, the thing that you need, of course."

From a corner of the cottage Old Magda snatched up a staff, some five feet long and as big around as her thumb. Calvin reached for it, but the witch thrust it at Ellen.

"The girl must carry it," said Old Magda. "The tea leaves are never wrong. Well, take it, lass. Take it!"

"But what's it for?" Ellen asked.

"How should I know?" Old Magda replied tartly. "Do you think I know everything? Just carry it with you, girl. And don't lose it. For that staff was hewn from the Coven Tree."

"The what?" asked Calvin.

"It's the old tree out by the crossroads that our village was named for," said Ellen. "Covens—groups of witches—used to meet under its branches. It's a spooky old tree, and it's said to have magic powers."

"Maybe the staff will aid you . . ." said Old Magda.

"Oh, thank you!" said Ellen.

". . . and maybe it won't. There are no guarantees in the fortune-telling business." The witch put a hand to her head. "I must lie down. Peering through that glass made me giddy. Please come again, Calvin."

The witch glanced at Ellen and wrinkled her scrawny nose. "And next time, come alone."

Old Magda collapsed onto her narrow cot. Calvin and Ellen tiptoed out of the cottage and started back toward town.

"Did you hear the way that old hag talked to me, Calvin?" snorted Ellen. "And you just stood there. You could have said something."

"It didn't seem proper," replied Calvin. "After all, we were there to get her help. I had to be polite, didn't I?"

"Not all *that* polite," said Ellen. "With all that fuss she was making over you, I felt like the fifth wheel on a hay wagon."

"There you go, getting uppity again. Here, let me see that staff."

Ellen snatched it out of his reach. "Old Magda said *I* was to have it. I ain't letting loose of it for anything."

"But . . ."

"No, I said."

Arguing loudly over who'd hold the staff, they trudged back toward Coven Tree.

CHAPTER SEVEN

The Black Knight

Calvin crouched in a dark corner of the garret of the Coven Tree general store. Through the open door at the far end of the garret he could see the great wooden beam that stuck out beyond the edge of the building, with its hanging tackle of ropes and pulleys that enabled one person to hoist heavy barrels and boxes up into the garret until they were needed in the store below. To the west were the mountains, with the setting sun just touching their tops.

The hinges of the trapdoor behind him creaked loudly as it was pushed from below. "Who's there?" he called in a frightened whisper.

"Calvin, is that you?" came the reply.

"Ellen?" Calvin let his breath out with a rush. "What are you doing here?"

"I followed you. Why are you hiding away like this?"

"It was Stew Meat's idea. Nobody can give me away to Dr. Dredd if they don't know where I am. But you'd best go, Ellen. It will be dangerous if Dredd finds me here."

Ellen shook her head. "I'm staying, Calvin. I want to be here with you if Dredd comes looking. I have the staff Old Magda gave me. I thought it might help."

"Hmmph," Calvin snorted. "A piece of wood isn't going to do much for me."

"Look, Calvin! People are gathering in the street below. They'll help you."

Calvin crept over to the open door and peered out. The main street of Coven Tree was filled with people, and more were arriving even as he watched. They overflowed onto yards and porches. From the garret high up in the store, they looked like a great mass of tiny animals, many of them wearing straw hats or poke bonnets. Some of the younger men were tying big torches to trees and buildings.

"All that because of me," said Calvin in an awed voice.

"They're carrying pitchforks and flails and clubs," said Ellen. "A few of 'em even have guns. Now Dredd won't dare . . ."

"He'll be here, of a certainty," said Calvin.

The sun sank below the distant hills. Night came across Coven Tree like a huge blanket. Suddenly a pair of screaming girls burst out of the woods and rushed up to Sheriff Houck.

"Rosalie and Barbara Raskind," said Ellen. "Nobody else can screech like that."

"We seen 'em!" Calvin heard Rosalie squeal.

"They was awful-lookin'," added Barbara.

"Calm down, you two," Sheriff Houck ordered. "What did you see?"

"Those two . . . *things*! They came right out of the woods and past our house."

"One was tall and skinny," said Barbara. "He had on a red hat. But the other . . . the other . . ."

"The other one was done up in an iron suit," gasped Rosalie. "Had a big sword in his hand, he did. He took a swipe at the boulder at the side of the path, and the sword sliced through it like it was cheese instead of stone."

The crowd began babbling loudly. Calvin saw one or two of the people slip off into the night.

Sheriff Houck turned to the mass of people. "Dredd's coming!" he bawled. "Light the torches!"

Matches flared, and one after another the torches were lit. They flickered and smoked, and the street was filled with an eerie light.

Then a single huge cry of astonishment came from the mob of people. Several of them pointed toward the end of the street.

There stood Dr. Dredd. Alone. The crowd suddenly fell silent.

"I want the boy!" Dredd cried, and his voice echoed from the nearby hills. "Give me Calvin Huckabee!"

Sheriff Houck left the safety of the crowd and strode toward Dredd. "You can't have him," the sheriff said firmly. "D'you think you can fight us all? Do you think you have that much power?"

"Power?" Dredd's laugh was an awful cackle. "I have power beyond your wildest dreams, Sheriff Houck."

"Then why don't you make the rain yourself instead of depending on Calvin Huckabee for it?"

"Rain is a thing of goodness and life," Dredd replied. "But mine is the power of death and destruction! Of fire . . ."

Dredd raised a bony hand. All at once sheets of fire criss-crossed the sky, one after another. Each one lit up the town brighter than midmorning and blasted the crowd with withering heat. Dredd lowered his hand and the flames ceased.

". . . of whirlwind . . ."

Again his hand shot upward. A great wind sprang from nowhere, whipping at the garments of the men and women, rattling windows all over town and ripping shingles from the roofs of buildings.

". . . of earthquake . . ."

The ground rumbled, and a huge crack appeared between the sheriff and the multitude of people. Calvin and Ellen could feel the entire store quivering beneath their feet. Dredd brought his hand down. The shaking ceased and the crack closed.

"Speak to me not of power, Sheriff Houck," said Dredd with a sneer. "If I wished, I could topple all of Coven Tree before your heart beats five more times. Now, where is the boy?"

"I . . . I don't know," said the sheriff. "None of us do."

Dredd peered into Houck's eyes. "You speak the truth," he said finally. "So I shall have to take steps to find him."

"I'm warning you, Dredd. Most everyone in town is here, and some of 'em have got guns. And from what Mrs. McCabe told me, you're afraid of guns."

"You won't shoot me, Sheriff," scoffed Dredd. "The law, as well as your silly conscience, won't allow it. As yet I've done nothing to warrant being killed."

"Then what . . ."

"Does a prince clean his own stables?" Dredd asked. "Does a great lord dispose of his own rubbish or care for his own horses and cattle? No, that is servants' work. I too have servants to do what is beneath me. Perhaps you would like to meet one of them."

Dredd took a tiny silver whistle from his pocket and put it to his lips. He blew one note into the still night air. Then he walked out of the village and into the forest.

While everyone was gaping at the spot where Dredd had disappeared among the trees, something else appeared at the edge of the village. Huge and monstrous, it glittered darkly in the torchlight. The great sword in its hand swung back and forth with a dreadful swishing sound.

Then Dredd's voice was heard from the darkness. "Find me Calvin Huckabee, you people of Coven Tree. Otherwise the Black Knight will seek him out and lay waste your town in the process!"

The Black Knight strode closer. Sheriff Houck dodged behind a tree at the edge of the road. "Stay away from me, you walking junkyard!" he cried.

The great sword hissed through the air. There was a loud *THUNK*. The tree behind which the sheriff was hiding began to topple to the ground. The knight had severed it with a single swipe of its sword.

Sheriff Houck cowered down behind the stump, afraid for his life. But the armored figure turned and advanced toward the mob in the street.

Cries of terror came from the crowd. Somebody

heaved a pitchfork but it fell short. A heavy oak club flew end-over-end toward the knight. He parried it with his sword.

BANG A gun was fired. The bullet struck the armor, bounced off and went whirring into the woods. A couple more shots rang out, sounding like corn popping. One of them pierced the knight's helmet, dead center.

"That'll fix him!" shouted someone.

But the Black Knight brushed at the hole in its helmet the way a man might brush away an annoying insect. It kept on coming.

Almost as one, the crowd broke and ran, retreating from the huge sword. Shouts of alarm and terror rang out. Two or three of the younger men tried to shinny up the posts in front of the village hall to escape. One of them lost his grip and fell back among the throng of people in the street. Ogden Thurlough tripped and would have been trampled underfoot if Doc Rush and Adam Fiske hadn't dragged him to safety. For perhaps twenty or thirty seconds Coven Tree's main street resembled an anthill that'd had boiling water poured into it. Men, women and even a few children were scurrying everywhere—anywhere—to escape that awful sword.

Then . . . stillness. The street, save for the Black Knight, was as deserted as if Coven Tree were a ghost town.

Dr. Dredd strode out of the woods and into the light. "Calvin Huckabee!" he called out. "I know you're within the sound of my voice. Come out now if you would save this town!"

"You stay put, Calvin," Ellen whispered in his ear.

"I'm losing patience!" Dredd cried in a menacing voice. He waited a moment longer. The silence was like a great cloud hanging over the village.

"Very well." Dredd snapped his fingers at the Black Knight. Then he pointed toward the stone firehouse at one end of the street.

With great strides the knight walked to one corner of the firehouse. It raised the sword high.

CLANG CLANG The sword struck sparks from the stone wall of the firehouse, slicing through it and tearing out huge chunks of rock and mortar. Soon there was a hole large enough for a horse and wagon to pass through.

"By morning, every building in Coven Tree will be reduced to rubble!" called Dredd. "Is that what you want, Calvin?"

"I can't let that happen," Calvin told Ellen. "I've got to go down there."

"No, Calvin! That . . . that thing will kill you!"

He shook his head. "I don't think so. Dredd needs me for the rain. Besides, I've got an idea."

He began whispering in Ellen's ear. "D'you really think it'll work?" she asked fearfully.

"It's got to. Now, I'm going to grab hold of the rope on the pulley block there. You lower me down, real careful."

Calvin grasped the rope at the end of the block and swung out into space. Ellen began letting out the line slowly. It wasn't as hard as she'd thought it would be. The rope creaked over the pulley wheels, and Calvin was lowered to the ground.

Finally the strain on the pulleys slacked off. "I'm down," came Calvin's whisper from below. "Now if I can fix this thing just the way I want it . . ."

"Calvin, be careful."

Dr. Dredd must have heard Ellen. Suddenly he turned toward the store. He blew on his silver whistle, and the Black Knight ceased hewing at the firehouse.

"Calvin?" hissed Dredd.

"I'm here, Dr. Dredd. Over here by the store."

"Come out into the light, lad. Come out where I can see you."

"Why don't you come and get me?"

Dredd shook his head. "And you can play one of your pesky tricks? I'm not that foolish. The Black Knight will fetch you."

He signaled to the knight. It began advancing with sword raised. "No, you fool!" cried Dredd. "I want to capture the boy, not kill him."

The knight threw its sword to the ground. Dredd pointed toward the wall of the store. "Get him!"

Leaving the sword on the dusty street, the knight plodded forward. Its arms were extended, and a terrible groaning sound came from inside its helmet. Closer and closer it came to the boy crouched against the side of the building.

Calvin dodged to the right. So did the knight. Then left, with the knight following each move so quickly that Calvin had no chance of escape. Finally Calvin stood with his back against the store's wall. The Black Knight loomed over him, legs spread wide and arms clutching.

As the Black Knight bent forward to grasp him, Calvin suddenly threw himself to the ground and scuttled between the knight's armored legs. At the same time he yelled up at the doorway above.

"Pull, Ellen! Pull!"

Up in the garret Ellen pulled on the rope with all her might.

The rope screeched through the pulley blocks. The noose that Calvin had fashioned and concealed in the grass sprang out like a striking snake and wrapped itself around the Black Knight's legs. The knight managed to jerk one leg free before the slipknot tightened the circle of rope around the other ankle.

Ellen yanked harder. The knight, off balance now, crashed to the ground with a clang of metal plates.

Then, as Ellen continued to haul away on the pulley

line, the knight began rising into the air, upside down and suspended by one leg.

Finally, when the inverted helmet was six feet off the ground and the rest of the knight's armor stretched above him in the darkness, Calvin called out to Ellen. "That's enough. We've got him. Tie off your end of the line to something solid up there."

The Black Knight struggled desperately, like a hooked fish on the end of a line. Its steel fists banged against the side of the store, and one or two of the boards were stove in. But try as it would, it could not bend upward far enough to reach the rope that pinioned its ankle. The Black Knight was caught for fair.

With the danger gone for the moment, folks began drifting back into town almost as if they were trying to spite Dr. Dredd. Pretty soon the street was nearly as full as it had been before. Dredd retreated toward the other end of town.

"The Black Knight—hung up like a side of beef by a couple of . . . children!" he snarled in outrage. "But I shall return, you may count on that. And next time I shall bring such horror that neither you nor all the country 'round will prevail against me!"

"You're not getting away that easy!" cried Sheriff Houck. "C'mon, folks. Let's get him!"

Some of the braver villagers broke loose from the crowd and began running toward Dredd. Quickly he bent and scooped up a handful of loose dirt. As they approached he threw it at them, making a thick cloud of dust.

For a moment they were blinded. When the dust cleared, Dredd was nowhere to be seen.

"He got clean away," said the astonished sheriff. "But I doubt we've seen the last of him."

Mayor Phipps puffed his way up beside the sheriff and pointed at the Black Knight, still struggling and banging against the side of my store making a tinny racket. "What are we going to do with that, Roscoe?" the mayor asked.

Before the sheriff could answer, Ellen walked grimly out through the store's front door. She was still carrying the staff Old Magda had given her.

"Looks like I didn't need any witch's magic after all," she said. "But I wish I had Dr. Dredd here right now. I'd . . . I'd . . ."

In a fit of anger she hauled back Old Magda's staff,

dodged the knight's groping arms, and swatted the upside-down helmet as hard as she could. *BONG* went the armor.

A strange moaning came from deep inside it. The sound grew louder . . . louder. . . . Then suddenly it ceased.

CLANK The helmet tumbled to the ground. But the rest of the armor kept struggling to get free.

Ellen got down on her hands and knees and crept beneath it. She peered up into the hole where a man's head would have come out—if there'd been a man inside.

"Why, there's nothing in there!" she cried out in surprise.

With that, a shiver went through the armor. All the struggling ceased.

CLANK One arm piece fell off and came to rest beside the helmet.

CLANK CLANK CLANK Arm piece . . . chest plate . . . leg piece. . . . One part after another, the pieces of the armor fell away until only a single leg piece remained hanging from the rope.

Gingerly, Sheriff Houck picked up bit after bit of

the armor and looked inside. "Empty as a dullard's head," he said finally.

"That's the Black Knight's secret!" exclaimed Ellen. "There is nothing to him except the armor itself. And as soon as anybody finds that out, the knight loses all its power."

"We done it!" Calvin yelled. "You and me. I'm so proud of you I could bust!"

"It was you who did all the dangerous stuff," Ellen replied, blushing in the torchlight.

"Sheriff," sputtered Mayor Phipps importantly, "get rid of that armor. Bury each piece of it separately throughout the village. After that, we'll have to send for some men and machines to fix the firehouse."

"Now, how are we going to do that, Eli?" asked the sheriff. "Like I told you earlier, the roads out of town are blocked, and the telegraph wire is down. All of us are being held prisoner in this village."

On hearing that, the mass of people gasped and one or two screams shattered the stillness.

"Calvin," said the mayor, "you know Dr. Dredd better'n anybody else. Isn't there anything we can do?"

"Do, Mayor Phipps?" said Calvin. "Cut off from the

outside world, and out there in the forest stalks a . . . a *thing* . . . that'll be wanting revenge for what we did to his Black Knight. Searching out Dr. Dredd would be as foolhardy as walking into a lion's den. So we're just going to have to wait until he shows up again."

"What'll we do then, Calvin?"

"About all I can think of is just hope and pray that nobody gets hurt real bad—or mebbe even killed!"

CHAPTER EIGHT

What's to Be Done?

The following morning found Ellen, her mother and Calvin in the McCabe living room. They'd all spent the night there, dozing uneasily on the sofa and easy chairs, not wanting to be caught alone and unaware if Dr. Dredd should show up again.

"I tell you, Ellen, I'm so angry with you that now I'm of two minds about Calvin's staying on here any longer," Mrs. McCabe was saying. "On the one hand, I've never in my life turned anybody who was in need away from my door. On the other hand—well, you could have been killed last night, Ellen. The very idea of running off after I'd told you to stick close to home!"

"I saw you in that crowd in town," replied Ellen. "You was carrying a pitchfork and yelling fit to bust."

"That's different," Mrs. McCabe snapped.

"How's it different, Mama? D'you mean it's all right for you to go off and defend the village, but I'm supposed to sit at home like some delicate flower? I'm too old for that kind of nonsense."

"You're getting to be a young woman, and that's a fact. But the difference is, I was trying to protect the village and all we've built up here. But you—well, all you could think about was running to be with Calvin the minute my back was turned."

Suddenly Calvin spoke up. " 'Scuse me, Mrs. McCabe," he said. "But I'm getting a mite tired of you two jawing away about me like I wasn't here at all. Fact is, Ellen wasn't in any danger up there in the garret. I was the one the Black Knight was after. I wouldn't put her at risk for anything. But if you want me to leave, I'll leave."

"Calvin, no!" Ellen cried out.

"An' mebbe Dr. Dredd will catch me, and mebbe he won't," Calvin went on. "If he does, he'll come back here, sure as shooting, to have me make it rain. Then he'll ruin this village just like all the others."

"Dr. Dredd ain't had much success in Coven Tree up to now," said Mrs. McCabe.

"No, ma'am. For he's got to provide a service before he can work his evil spells. Anyway, mebbe I can keep away from Dredd until he gets sick of looking for me. In that case I'll be coming back myself. Coven Tree is the first place I've found in years where people care whether I live or die. And I'd be proud to settle here, once I'm free of the Wagon of Wonders."

Mrs. McCabe rocked in her chair, looking from Calvin to Ellen and back again. "Oh, it's hard times in Coven Tree," she said with a sigh. "First the spring drought . . . then Dredd's coming . . . Sven Hensen's fight with Antaeus . . . the Black Knight . . ."

"What did they do with that armor, Mama?" asked Ellen, trying to change the subject. "Did they bury it all about, like Mayor Phipps ordered?"

Mrs. McCabe nodded. "All except the helmet. Sven Hensen said that with a little work on his part it could be shaped into a grand kettle. Kind of odd, thinking of apple butter or Irish stew being cooked up in that thing."

Then she fell silent, rocking stiffly back and forth. "Hard times," she repeated finally. "School's closed, and everybody's sticking close to home, shivering in their boots and knowing Dr. Dredd is out there. . . ."

Just then, there came a rapping at the front door. Mrs. McCabe picked up a big chunk of wood from the box by the fireplace and then got up from her chair. "If that's Dr. Dredd, I'll break his head with this," she said, waving the wood about. "I swear I will."

But when she peeked through the living room window, she saw only Sheriff Houck on the porch. "Come in, Sheriff," said Mrs. McCabe, flinging the door open wide. "What brings you here?"

"We're having a kind of special meeting at the church this evening."

"It's about Calvin, isn't it?" asked Ellen.

"Yes, Miss Ellen, it surely is. Up to last night, most everybody wanted to protect him, no matter what. But after seeing what Dredd is capable of doing, some folks are changing their minds. One idea is to take Calvin out in the woods somewhere and just leave him—mebbe tied to a tree—so's Dredd will perhaps go away and leave us in peace. A lot of others still feel Calvin's a part of the town now, and we shouldn't give in to Dredd, no matter what. I guess a meeting's the only way to get things settled."

"Why not have the meeting right now?" Ellen asked.

"I've got to be sure everybody's notified. That'll take most of the day. Then again, when darkness comes, people are going to be even more frightened than they are now. I reckon they'd feel better all gathered in one place. You three plan on being there, hear? And Calvin Huckabee, don't you try nothing foolish in the meantime."

By the time Calvin, Ellen and Mrs. McCabe got to the church that evening, the benches were filled and a lot of folks were standing in the aisles. But special seats had been saved way up in front since Calvin was kind of the guest of honor, as it were.

Reverend Terwilliger started the meeting with a prayer that said what I guess all of us had on our minds: " 'From ghoulies and ghosties and long-legged beasties and things that go bump in the night, Good Lord deliver us.' " Then he turned the meeting over to Sheriff Houck.

"I guess you all know," the sheriff began with a tug at his collar, "that there's a danger threatening our village. Since yesterday there's nobody come in from outside, and nobody here has been able to leave."

"You're talking like there was an army out there in the woods," hooted somebody, "instead of just one man."

"I ain't at all sure Dr. Hugo Dredd could be rightly called a man," said the sheriff. "For he seems to have powers beyond what mortals possess. Most of you saw examples of that last night. In any case, he wants something from us."

Mort Sweeney shot up off his bench and pointed an accusing finger at Calvin. "Dredd wants the boy!" he cried. "And I say we give him what he wants. That's the only way we'll be left in peace."

"Well, that's one point of view," replied Sheriff Houck. "But there are others, to be sure. Does anybody else want a say?"

Drusella Pritt raised a timid hand. "I've heard the

boy was whipped by Dr. Dredd," she said, "and got treated right cruelly. 'Twould be a shame to turn Calvin Huckabee back to such a creature."

Mrs. McCabe looked at Ellen and Calvin in surprise. "Well I never!" she said. "I always took Drusella to be the most cowardly woman ever put on this earth. And here she is defending you, Calvin. Will wonders never—"

But Miz Pritt hadn't finished. "Wouldn't it be just as well," she went on, "to have the boy leave town? Isn't that how you'd handle any undesirable person, Sheriff?"

Ellen McCabe rose from her place and fixed Drusella with an icy stare. "An' you just tell me, Drusella Pritt," she said scornfully, "what's so all-fired undesirable about Calvin. He don't parade around town all day, gossiping about the neighbors the way you do. And . . . and . . ."

Mrs. McCabe took hold of Ellen's arm and yanked her down into her place. "Stop that, Ellen. It ain't respectable."

"Respectable!" grumbled Ellen. "She knows blame well that sending Calvin off is the same as putting him in Dredd's lap. She wants credit for being charitable—but only if it don't cost her nothing."

"Now, that'll be enough outbursts," announced Sheriff Houck, taping on the pulpit with his knuckles. "Has anybody else got an idea?"

Everybody sat with bowed heads, sneaking looks about to see if one of the others was going to speak up. But nobody did. Up front, Mrs. McCabe whispered in Ellen's ear. "Now, not a word, girl. Calvin's special to us. But it's the rest of the village that'll have to decide what's to become of him."

Silence.

Well, if no one else would say anything, I guessed it was up to me. I'm not much of a speaker, but I was set on saying what I had on my mind. I raised my hand.

"Stew Meat," said the sheriff. "Your advice is usually well taken. What would you have us hear?"

I got slowly to my feet. Then I looked about at the sea of heads. "I reckon I came to the wrong place tonight," I began.

"What do you mean by that?" Mort Sweeney muttered. "Everybody in town is here, Stew Meat."

"Oh?" I replied. "Then mebbe I got the right place—but the wrong people. For I'd always thought the good folk of Coven Tree had a lot more sense—and a lot more courage—than I've seen here thus far."

"Stew Meat, are you accusing us of cowardice?" asked the sheriff. "You can't—"

"I'll say anything I've a mind to, Roscoe. Firstly, let's do some hard thinking about the reason we're gathered here tonight. We're deciding whether the boy, Calvin Huckabee, will be returned to Dr. Dredd or not. Right?"

There was a humming of agreement throughout the church.

"Now if we keep him," I went on, "Dr. Dredd's going to seek some horrible revenge. We know that. But let's say, for the moment, that we give Calvin up to Dredd. What then?"

"Why, Dredd will make him give us the rain we need," someone cried out.

"True. But he won't be doing it out of the goodness of his heart—if a creature like that has a heart to begin with. Oh, no! Once the rain's over, he'll seek to collect his part of the bargain. And it won't be money or goods.

We know now that he plans to do something evil to this town, and I have no doubt it'll destroy Coven Tree as surely as the earthquake or fire or whirlwind he brought last night. Perhaps it'll be slower than as if we kept the lad. But in the end it'll be just as sure. Coven Tree as we know it will be done."

"You mean . . . if we don't give Calvin up," said Mayor Phipps slowly, "we're doomed! And . . . and . . ."

"If we do send him back to Dredd, we're still doomed," finished Sheriff Houck.

"That's the size of it," I said, nodding in agreement. "And that brings me to my second point—courage!"

"Just having courage won't save us!" Sumner Beezum shouted out.

"Mebbe not. But by giving Calvin back, we'd be doing something as bad as Dredd himself is capable of. I think that here in Coven Tree, we've got more courage than to do a thing like that."

I paused and waited for some reply. None was forthcoming.

"I say we fight Dr. Hugo Dredd any way we can," I concluded. "If we win, we win. If not, and if Coven

Tree is leveled to the ground, then we will rebuild. But at least when all is done with, we'll be able to look one another in the eye and know what we did was right!"

With that, I sat down. All around me it was silent, and the quiet was almost thick enough to touch.

Then, off in a far corner, Packer Vickery lifted all three hundred pounds of himself to his feet. "Calvin Huckabee stays!" he announced positively. The bench creaked and groaned as he sat back down again.

"I reckon you'd better take your vote now, Sheriff Houck," called out Sumner Beezum. "As for me, I couldn't have said it any better'n Stew Meat did. The boy remains in Coven Tree. And as for Dr. Dredd, he can take a long leap into Spider Crick."

Suddenly a big hootin' and hollerin' began within the church. Some of the men went up front to shake Calvin's hand, and a couple of the ladies gave him big hugs that made his face get all red. There wasn't any question about how the vote would go.

Calvin could remain in Coven Tree as long as he liked.

It was just then that a big wind came whooshing through the open windows of the church. At the same time, every light in the place went out.

For a moment we all just sat there in the eerie darkness. The sheriff lit some candles on the altar so there'd be something to see by. That's when we heard the ghastly shrieks outside.

They rose in pitch and got louder, like the screams of an animal in awful pain. A few of us crept to the windows to see what was going on.

Outside, the moonlight shone down on the little graveyard beside the church. Suddenly from behind several of the tombstones rose dim figures that seemed to be made of fog and dust. They were terrible to look upon, with heads like skulls and hideous, twisted bodies. Slowly those creatures of the night advanced toward us. But just as they reached the open windows they turned aside, their ghastly cries ringing out as if nearing the church was painful.

Packer Vickery's teeth chattered in his head, and Drusella Pritt fell down in a dead faint. That's when the lights went back on and the great church door flew open with a loud bang.

In the doorway stood Dr. Dredd.

The red top hat was drawn low over his slits of eyes. In his left hand was a dirty leather sack, and the thing inside seemed to be heavy and smooth. He raised his right arm menacingly, and silence fell over the people.

Yet I noted that he remained in the doorway and made no attempt to enter the church. This heartened me, and I was the first to speak out.

"Quite a show you put on out there in the graveyard," I said. "Those demons and monsters must have come from the Dark Pit itself. I'd not thought even your powers were so . . ."

"You do me too much credit, Stew Meat," he replied in a mocking voice. "My master—Satan himself—has taken a keen in interest in the fate of Calvin Huckabee. It was Master who summoned up the creatures, not I. Just to give you people some idea of the great forces arrayed against you."

Suddenly his evil grin twisted into an expression of rage. His teeth champed together with a grinding sound, and in his eyes was the look of a madman.

"I've come for the boy!" he roared, and his voice echoed from the rafters.

It was then that Reverend Terwilliger showed the kind of heart he had. He stepped behind the pulpit, glared down the long aisle, and pointed a finger at Dredd.

"No!" he cried out. "You shall not have him! We are all of a mind on this. So do your worst, sir. We're prepared for whatever befalls us."

"Then you're fools!" cried Dredd as he stomped his foot on the threshold. "For this time I will have my way in this. You'll see."

"Wait," I said, for I wanted to test the extent of Dredd's powers. "Perhaps, Dr. Dredd, you'd like to come inside and put your case to these good people. Clear the way for him there."

Those who were standing in the aisle moved to the side so Dredd had a clear path to the pulpit. But still he made no move to enter the church. He looked around, and it seemed to me that for the first time I saw fear flicker in his eyes.

"I prefer to do my debating from here, Stew Meat," he replied. So I knew that for the moment at least, we were safe. Dr. Dredd could not enter a church, no more than could any other of the Devil's spawn.

"What gives you the right to have Calvin Huckabee?" I asked.

"I took him from the orphanage when no one else would have him," answered Dredd. "He's mine, to do with as I will."

"This is not a table we speak of, Dredd, nor a shoe or a mirror or some other bit of property. This is a human being."

"Bah! You talk of humans as if they were something special, storekeeper."

"And you speak of Calvin Huckabee as if he were a mere tool for some plot you have against this village. Why do you go to such lengths to get the boy back?"

A ghastly grin spread across Dredd's face. "No harm in telling," he said, "for there's naught you can do to save yourselves now. You people of Coven Tree made a bargain with me—a covenant. I was to bring rain. In return, I was to receive a fee which, at the time, I did not clearly spell out."

"Just what is that fee?" I asked.

"I will plant a small seed in the heart and mind of each of you," Dredd replied. "And its name will be *Greed*. At first it will be small. But it will grow, as surely as do the pine trees on the hillsides. Finally it will possess each of you completely. Day in and day out, you will each have but a single thought: *I . . . want . . . MORE!*

"Gone will be charity and respect and love. Gone, the willingness to help one another in adversity. Gone, obedience to the law and concern for the respect of others. There will remain only those three words, blotting out all that is good and fine and decent: *I . . . want . . . MORE!*"

"That man is the Devil himself!" a woman cried out.

Dredd removed his hat and bowed low. "I thank you for the compliment, madam," he said with a mocking laugh. "My Master will be pleased to know of your good opinion of me. All of you, think on what I have said. Think of neighbor pitted against neighbor, friend against friend, husband against wife—all seeking personal advantage, no matter what the cost. Coven Tree will become . . . well, a place that my Master would be proud of. And even now, knowing my plan, there isn't anything you can do to prevent it. Once Calvin Huckabee makes the rain you thought you needed above all else . . ."

"We will not allow you to have him!" Reverend Terwilliger cried out.

Dredd looked around at the people assembled in the church. Many of the faces were pale and frightened. Yet they looked back at him without flinching.

"So say you all?" Dredd asked in a sneering voice.

There were murmurs of assent throughout the church.

"You have your answer, Dr. Dredd," said Reverend Terwilliger from the pulpit. "Now begone, sir."

"Not quite yet, I think. You will regret what you do this night." Dredd stooped down and reached into his leather sack with both hands. When he straightened again, he was holding the dragon's black egg before him.

"The thing inside this egg is mine to command," he said loudly. "It will seek out the boy, wherever he may be. Come between me and what is rightfully mine, and Coven Tree and its people will be wiped away like a puff of smoke in a gale!"

With that, Dredd raised the egg high above his head and then sent it crashing down onto the stone steps of the church.

A single white crack appeared along its black surface. The crack began to widen. Reverend Terwilliger sprang down from the pulpit and started along the center aisle.

"Beware!" Dredd warned.

Before Reverend Terwilliger could reply, a loud cry came from within the egg. In that cry we heard the piercing shriek of the hawk and the roar of the lion and the shrill scream of a soul in torment. At the same time, a flickering light came from the crack as if the inside of the egg had burst into flame.

The egg cracked fully open. Something crawled out of it. The thing was perhaps two feet long, with scaly, lizardlike skin. A long tail with a spike at its end lashed back and forth, and when the thing's mouth opened, we could see fangs along both jaws. Wings uncurled from the creature's shoulders, and the claws of its feet scratched against the stone steps.

Suddenly we heard the unearthly cry again. At the same time, flame spewed from the monster's maw.

"Look!" cried Sumner Beezum, pointing a finger. "It's growing!"

Indeed it was. Even as we watched, the thing got

larger until it was twice its original size. Dredd pointed into the darkness and uttered some words that nobody understood.

The dragon, as if following orders, scuttled off toward the dark forest.

"I would ask you to reconsider your decision to protect the boy," said Dredd with a smirk. "But now it's too late. Even as the minutes pass the dragon gets bigger and bigger. I wonder how many of you will be alive tomorrow to see the sun come up over what's left of Coven Tree."

With that, he vanished into the night.

For a moment we were all struck dumb by what we'd seen. Then, from the front of the church, we heard a loud shout.

"No!" cried Calvin Huckabee. "I can't let this happen!"

Before anybody could stop him, he raced down the aisle and out of the church.

"Calvin, wait!" shouted Ellen McCabe. Her mother tried to grasp her arm, but she twisted free and scurried toward the rear door.

"Calvin!"

Then she too was gone.

Somebody banged the doors closed and shot the bolts. I made my way to the front of the church where Mrs. McCabe was weeping loudly. “What will become of them, Stew Meat?” she sobbed. “Calvin and . . . and Ellen? What will become of them . . . ?”

We just didn’t know.

CHAPTER NINE

Fiery Pursuit

Old Baldy is the highest of the peaks that surround Coven Tree. Halfway up its pine-covered side is a small cabin, built to shelter hikers who might be overtaken by darkness or storms. Only at its very top do the trees and underbrush give way to a dome of solid rock that gives the mountain its name.

It was toward Old Baldy that Calvin Huckabee ran after darting out of the Coven Tree church. Once he reached the base he began climbing, heedless of the dry branches that slashed and raked at his face and body. Although the full moon was bright in the sky, only a tiny part of its light reached down through the trees to the forest floor.

Frightened near to panic, Calvin had only one purpose in his flight. He wanted to get as far away from Coven Tree as he could.

He stopped for a moment to catch his breath. Somewhere in the darkness below him, he heard a dry branch snap.

Upward—ever upward—he climbed. Then he heard a rock, dislodged from its place, roll away. The sound was nearer now. Whatever the ghastly thing pursuing him, it was catching up.

Calvin groped about the forest floor, feeling prickly pine needles under his fingers. His hand brushed a fallen limb. He jerked at it. The limb was a long one, and he gripped it with both hands. It wasn't much of a weapon, but at least he wouldn't give up without a struggle.

He dodged behind a great pine tree and pressed as close as he could to its trunk. The bark was rough against his cheek. Then he spread his feet and lifted the limb high over his head, ready to strike.

There was a crackling sound of footsteps coming closer. Funny, thought Calvin. A dragon ought to make more noise than that. Perhaps it had padded feet or something. Calvin hadn't had any experience with dragons.

Whatever was pursuing him was almost near enough to touch now. A shadowy figure, dim in the filtered moonlight, passed the tree behind which he was hiding.

"Now I got you!" yelled Calvin. The tree limb whistled through the air.

"Calvin, don't!" cried a shrill voice.

The shadow fell to one side, and Calvin's club thumped harmlessly into the dry, papery leaves of the forest floor.

"Ellen, is that you?"

"Course it is. Here, come help me up."

Calvin took her arm and helped her to her feet. "What are you doing here?" he demanded.

"I had to come, Calvin. I just had to. I couldn't let you run off all alone."

"You get yourself back down the mountain where

you'll be safe," said Calvin. "There's no reason for both of us . . . I mean . . ."

"I know every inch of this mountain, Calvin, and you don't. Without me you'll just run about aimlessly until Dr. Dredd catches up with you."

"I'll be just fine. Chances are he'll never find me in all this forest."

But Calvin knew better. So did Ellen.

"No. I know now that he'll find you though you travel to the ends of the earth," she told him sadly. "It's time to face up to his evil."

"I'll think of something to do, Ellen. But I want you safe. Go home now."

"I can't."

"Why can't you?"

"Look."

Ellen pointed down the side of the mountain. At first Calvin saw nothing but darkness. Then, there it was again. A spout of flame that spiraled upward like a hundred torches burning at once.

"Dragon's breath," said Ellen. "You wouldn't send me back down with that waiting, would you, Calvin?"

"In this dry weather, Dredd could set the whole

mountain ablaze. I reckon there's nothing for it but to keep climbing. Consarn it, Ellen! Why'd you have to do such a fool thing as runnin' after me?"

"This ain't the time to start arguing, Calvin Huckabee. There's an old cabin a little way up the mountain. Maybe we can hide there until Dredd passes us by."

Fifteen minutes more of climbing brought them before the shadowly outline of a crude cabin. They groped their way inside and slammed the door after them, bolting it tight. Slivers of moonbeams coming through the window at the rear of the hut were the only light.

Silence. Calvin heard nothing but the sound of his own heartbeat and the frightened breathing of Ellen close beside him. Five minutes passed. . . . Ten . . .

Then Dr. Dredd's awful cry came from somewhere in the darkness outside. "Calvin Huckabee! I know you're in there. And the girl, too. Come out, I say!"

Calvin darted to the cabin's door and peered through a small chink between two of the boards. He saw nothing but darkness.

Then a single blast of fire lit up the whole clearing in front of the cabin. In the light of the flames Calvin Huckabee saw the stuff of nightmares.

"El—El—Ellen!" he gasped. "Look!"

Ellen pressed her eye to the crack in the door. "Calvin, I don't see anything but . . ."

Another roaring stream of fire issued from the dragon's mouth. By its light she saw Dr. Dredd, his tiny eyes red with anger. But it was the thing beside him that made Ellen McCabe's blood run cold within her.

It was more than twenty feet long and as high at the shoulder as a horse. The tremendous lizard was covered with scales, each as large as a silver dollar, and beneath its skin, muscles bulged and stretched. Its legs, each as big as a tree trunk, ended in feet from which long pointed claws slashed at the ground. The lashing tail, thick as a hogshead at its base, swept the earth and thumped against the nearby trees. Great wings sprouted from its back, flapping the air like leathery sails.

The dragon's head was the most horrible. Eyes the size of soup bowls stared evilly at the cabin. The snout of a nose sucked in air with loud whooshing sounds. The dreadful forked tongue probed out as if searching for something.

The head tilted back until the mouth pointed at the

sky. With a roar, a spout of flame shot out of the monster's throat and rose high in the air.

"My little pet," called Dredd, "has grown to full size now, though it needs practice in using its wings. Deliver yourself up to me, Calvin Huckabee. Otherwise you and the girl will die in a manner most horrible."

"We're done for," groaned Calvin.

"You have one minute," Dredd announced. "Then I'll command the dragon to destroy you both."

"Calvin, don't just stand there!" cried Ellen from the rear of the cabin. "Help me get this window open."

Calvin raced to where Ellen was pushing at the window. "It's stuck," she said.

"Thirty seconds, Calvin," called Dredd.

"It's moving," Ellen panted. "Hurry!"

Slowly the rotting window slid upward. Quickly Calvin lifted Ellen into the air and slid her through the opening. Then he followed, landing heavily on the ground outside. "Now, run!" Ellen snapped.

They ran. Upward, ever upward.

"Time's up," Dredd announced from below. He called out something in a language neither Calvin nor Ellen understood.

The dragon's head reared back on its long neck. Then the head shot forward. Fire spouted from its mouth like water from a thick hose and engulfed the cabin. The building exploded into flames that shot up to the sky and started smaller blazes in the trees alongside.

"Keep moving," said Calvin to Ellen, who was staring horrified at the burning cabin. "Those dry trees will burn in no time. Now we've got not only Dredd and the dragon but a forest fire to escape from."

Before she could reply, a roar of outrage came from Dr. Dredd. "They're gone! After them!"

Higher and higher Ellen and Calvin climbed. Then, suddenly, they were no longer plodding through thick pine forest but were walking on hard rock. They saw the sides of Old Baldy sloping away around them.

They had reached the top of the mountain.

The full moon, now halfway to the horizon, lit up the whole rocky summit. "No place to hide up here," Ellen said. "We'd best start down the other side."

Without another word they scrambled across the rock toward the wall of forest at the far end of the clearing. But before they could reach it there was a

tremendous roar and a great light as the trees in front of them burst into sheets of flame.

"The dragon!" Calvin cried out. "Dredd must have circled around and come up in front of us. Quick, Ellen! Back the other way!"

They raced back the way they'd come. But just as they were about to slip into the forest a hideous figure stepped out from among the trees.

"I sent my dragon on ahead of you," said Dr. Dredd triumphantly. "I thought you'd try something like this. So which will it be? Me? Or the dragon's fiery breath?"

"All right," said Calvin, and in his voice was all the misery of his situation. "Just let Ellen go and I'll come with you with no complaint."

"You're in no position to dictate terms, Calvin Huckabee," said Dredd with a chuckle. "Come here, girl."

He gripped Ellen's wrist in one bony claw of a hand. Then he began dragging her across the rock toward where the dragon was slithering into the clearing.

"Run, Calvin, run!" Ellen screamed. "Now's your chance!"

"He'll not run," said Dredd.

As much as Calvin wanted to escape, he knew it

was true. He just couldn't leave Ellen in Dredd's clutches. But what was there left to do? How could he combat the flaming breath of the dragon?

Just one way.

Calvin threw himself to the ground, resting his head against the cool rock. In his mind flashed images of Dr. Dredd drowning in a pool of mud and being swept away by a raging river and struggling amid great ocean waves with no land in sight. Calvin felt the pain slash through his head until he thought his skull would shatter.

At the same time, the power within him reached out to the skies above.

A thick, boiling mass of clouds began to gather over the summit of Old Baldy. This would be no small rain. This would have to be a hundred . . . a *thousand* . . . times greater than the worst storm he'd ever created. He needed torrents of rain, waterfalls of rain, gushers of rain—no matter that the agony inside his head might drive him mad or even kill him.

SPUTT The first drop of rain fell. Then another and another. In the sky above, the massive pile of clouds seethed, and ominous rumbles of thunder echoed from the rocks and forests. Within seconds the rain was teeming down, flowing and burbling across the rocks and gurgling into the earth of the forest. The fire on the other side of the clearing hissed into darkness, as did the one lower down around the cabin. Steam rose into the night air, and Calvin smelled the stink of charred wood.

In the center of the clearing Dr. Dredd stood before the huge dragon, holding Ellen captive beside him.

Then, above the claps of thunder, Calvin heard a sound that chilled his soul and filled him with despair.

Dr. Dredd was laughing at him.

CHAPTER TEN

Good-bye Forever

Back down in the valley—in Coven Tree—us folks had been doing some searching for Calvin and Ellen. Truth is, though, we'd been doing it pretty close to the church, just in case Dr. Dredd should return.

Suddenly Sumner Beezum pointed toward Old Baldy. "Look!" he shouted.

A bit more than halfway up the side of the mountain—just about where the old cabin stood—a fire had broken out.

"You take some men and gather tools, Stew Meat," said the sheriff. "Picks, shovels, water tanks—the whole kit and kaboodle. I'll organize the rest into fire-fighting teams. As dry as it is, that blaze could burn for miles."

"But Dr. Dredd . . ." somebody protested.

"Oh, hang Dr. Dredd! If that fire spreads, there won't be enough left of Coven Tree to dust a fiddle with!"

We'd just about gotten ourselves organized when we saw the storm coming up. For the most part the night was still and calm, with a big full moon off to the west. But just above the top of Old Baldy hung an inky mass of clouds, twisting and churning like something alive. We could see lightning flashes within the clouds, and the faint sound of thunder came to our ears. The flames around the old cabin got smaller and smaller until finally they disapeared altogether.

"That'll be Calvin Huckabee's doing, for sure," I told Sheriff Houck. "He and Ellen need help. We'd best get up there."

The sheriff shouted to the men to come along and bring their tools for weapons. Several of the women decided to go, too. Judging from the looks on their faces, Dr. Dredd was going to have a mighty hard time if they ever caught up with him.

High on Old Baldy's peak, Dr. Dredd's whoops of insane laughter crashed into Calvin's ears in great waves of ridicule. "Do you think all your rain can turn me from my purpose or put out my dragon's fire, you foolish boy?" Dredd jeered. "Go on, do your worst. Bring rain until your head bursts from the agony of it. And when you're done you'll still be my slave!"

"Just . . . don't . . . harm . . . Ellen!" gasped Calvin. "She's done nothing."

"At the gate of my Master's realm in the stygian depths of Hades," cried Dredd, "certain words appear in letters as black as sin. They read: ***ALL HOPE ABANDON, YE WHO ENTER HERE!*** You, Calvin Huckabee, are about to realize the full import of that message. I want you to understand forever that you are mine, to do with as I will. It wouldn't do to have you constantly dreaming of Ellen McCabe and of what might have been. The girl will be destroyed, and that's the end of it!"

"No!" screamed Calvin.

Even as his body twisted and contorted in anguish, and wave after wave of pain rocketed through it, Calvin increased the storm's fury. Flashes of red lanced across his vision as he watched Dr. Dredd haul Ellen to a spot in front of the dragon. She stood there as if mesmerized while Dredd walked to one side, pointed at her and barked a command to the dragon in strange words.

The dragon lurched back and then reared up on its massive hind legs. Its huge head and fiery maw loomed above Dredd. The wicked eyes peered intently at Ellen.

Dredd barked another command into the stormy night. The dragon drew back its head like a snake preparing to strike. As the rain came sheeting down, the great beast took a deep breath. Air roared into its open mouth.

Then there came from the clouds above a deafening sound that began like the tearing of tremendous sheets of cloth. Close upon that was a great, earth-shattering boom louder than all the cannons in the world. The very stones of the mountain shook and trembled. At the same time the whole clearing was bathed in a light brighter than midday sun.

The bolt of lightning arced out of the clouds like an enormous white-hot lance. It struck the dragon full on top of its upraised head. Then it sparked along the body, outlining wings, claws and scaled skin with pure brightness.

From the dragon, the bolt leapt to Dr. Dredd himself, striking him in the center of his back and smashing him to the ground like a swatted fly. Then the lightning crashed to the rocks beneath, shattering them and opening wide cracks.

A single despairing cry echoed in the darkness and silence that followed. But whether it came from Dr. Dredd or his great monster, Calvin couldn't tell.

Slowly the dragon toppled backward in the moonlight. It thudded heavily to the ground and lay still, its wings crushed beneath its massive body. A plume of steam escaped from between clenched fangs. Slowly the huge tail lifted high into the air and then slammed down onto the rock.

The awful creature was dead.

Ellen shook her head and rubbed her eyes. Though still half dazed, she spotted Calvin at the far end of the clearing and ran to where he lay.

"Look, Calvin!" she shouted suddenly. "Dredd's moving!"

Across the clearing, Dr. Dredd's body suddenly jerked to its feet like a puppet when the strings are pulled. He was surrounded by an eerie glow, and sparks shot from his fingertips. His coat was torn and charred down the back, and his red hat had a big dent in it.

"He can't be . . . alive," Calvin mumbled through the pain that made his head feel like a ball of molten steel. "The 'lectricity from the lightning's jerking his muscles, that's all."

"Are you sure?" asked Ellen, terrified.

"Gotta . . . be . . . that. I can't do no more . . . no more . . ."

While the sparks of lightning sizzled about him, Dredd began quivering all over like a person with the ague. Then he seemed to shrink in upon himself. One moment he stood there the height of a man, and the next, he was only as tall as a boy. Smaller he became, and smaller still. He shrank to the size of a groundhog and then tinier than a chipmunk. His red hat slipped down over his ears . . . his head . . . his shoulders . . . until finally it covered him completely.

Calvin fainted. The rain began to let up.

Ellen made her way across the rock to where Dredd's red hat sat on the ground. She lifted it. Underneath was nothing but a tiny pile of white dust.

"Good-bye forever, Dr. Dredd," she said with a smile of satisfaction. She blew on the dust, and it whirled off into the darkness, leaving only a small smudge on the wet rock.

Then she scurried back to Calvin, afraid of what she'd find. His eyes were closed, and he lay as still as death. He breathed in little gasps, and his heart beat weakly in his chest.

"It's all over, Calvin," she whispered, cradling his head in her lap. "You can't die now. We've won."

That's how we found things when our rescue party reached the summit of Old Baldy the following morning. We all marveled at the dragon's body, but nobody dared get too near it even though it was dead. Dr. Dredd's red hat stood beside it, and we all thought it best to leave things as they were up there on the mountain. The sooner Coven Tree was rid of Dr. Dredd, the better.

As we came down from the mountain, we took turns carrying Calvin. Sven Hensen toted Ellen the whole way, with her protesting that she was all right. Mrs. McCabe walked alongside and clucked about how the blacksmith should handle her gently and take care not to slip in the thick mud underfoot.

Needless to say, Calvin Huckabee recovered just fine. And he told all of Coven Tree the tale of what happened up there on Old Baldy, just as I've set it down here.

About a week afterward, Uncle Poot the dowser man was doing some exploring down there where the deep woods meet Fletcher's Bog. Came across a wagon, he did—same kind as Dr. Dredd had. Only the one Uncle Poot found was all rotten and moldering and falling to pieces like it had been there a hundred years or so. Through one of the busted windows Uncle Poot saw cupboards and tables. There was nothing on any of them except little piles of dust.

And Calvin? He meant what he'd said about staying on in Coven Tree. He goes to school regular, and during his free time he supports himself by doing odd jobs that nobody else seems able to handle right. Whether it's a horse with spavin or a clock that won't keep proper time or a henhouse that needs to be made safe against marauding foxes, Calvin seems to know just what to do.

'Course, it annoys some people that the McCabe household always seems to have first call on his services just when he's needed elsewhere. But I guess you can figure out why that is.

Rain? No, Calvin don't make it rain anymore. At least that's what he says. But somehow, just when it's needed most, a shower or two does come along through Coven Tree, and then the farmers are happy. Those times, Calvin doesn't do work of any kind.

That's when you'll find him at home.

Nursing a headache.

About the Author

Bill Brittain enjoys writing books in which playfully mysterious forces are afoot. *The Wish Giver*, a 1984 Newbery Honor Book, is set in Coven Tree—a town where wishes come true. *Devil's Donkey*, a companion volume to *The Wish Giver*, also takes place in Coven Tree. Both of these books were named ALA Notable Children's Books, as well as *School Library Journal* Best Books. In Mr. Brittain's first book, *All the Money in the World*, a boy captures a leprechaun who grants him three wishes. The book won the 1982-1983 Charlie May Simon Children's Book Award and was adapted for television as an ABC-TV Saturday Special. And his most recent book, the fast-paced mystery *Who Knew There'd Be Ghosts?*, was a Children's Choice for 1986 (IRA/CBC).

Mr. Brittain is also the author of over 65 mystery stories that have appeared in *Ellery Queen's Mystery Magazine*, *Alfred Hitchcock's Mystery Magazine* and several anthologies. He and his wife, Ginny, live in Asheville, North Carolina.

About the Artist

Andrew Glass is a well-known illustrator of fantasy and adventure stories for young readers. In addition to his drawings for *Dr. Dredd's Wagon of Wonders*, he has illustrated its companion volumes, *Devil's Donkey* and *The Wish Giver*; *Banjo* by Robert Newton Peck; *Spooky Night* by Natalie Savage Carlson; and the 1983 Newbery Honor Book *Graven Images* by Paul Fleischman. Mr. Glass is also the author and illustrator of two picture books: *Jackson Makes His Move* and *My Brother Tries to Make Me Laugh*. He lives and works in New York City.